SUBTERRANE

A NOVEL

Valérie Bah

ESPLANADE BOOKS

THE FICTION IMPRINT AT VÉHICULE PRESS

Published with the generous assistance of the Canada Council for the Arts, the Canada Book Fund of the Department of Canadian Heritage, and the Société de développement des entreprises culturelles du Québec (SODEC).

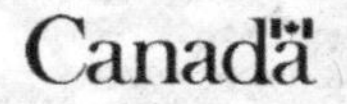

SODEC Québec

Canada Council for the Arts Conseil des arts du Canada

Esplanade Books editor: Dimitri Nasrallah
Cover design: David Drummond
Typeset in Minion and Gill Sans MT by Simon Garamond
Printed by Marquis Imprimeur

Dépôt légal, Library and Archives Canada and
Bibliothèque nationale du Québec, third quarter 2024

Library and Archives Canada Cataloguing in Publication

Title: Subterrane : a novel / Valérie Bah.
Names: Bah, Valérie, author.
Identifiers: Canadiana (print) 20240400496 | Canadiana (ebook) 20240405609 | ISBN 9781550656671 (softcover) | ISBN 9781550656718 (EPUB)
Subjects: LCGFT: Humorous fiction. | LCGFT: Novels.
Classification: LCC PS8603.A4415 S83 2024 | DDC C813/.6—dc23

Published by Véhicule Press, Montréal, Québec, Canada

Distribution in Canada by LitDistCo
www.litdistco.ca

Distribution in US by Independent Publishers Group
www.ipgbook.com

Printed in Canada on FSC® - certified paper.

CONTENTS

DRAMATIS PERSONAE

New Stockholm

Zeynab	the artist
Maya	a witness to Zeynab
Chekhov	a feline and runaway
Frantz	a lothario and expellee of Cipher Falls

Cipher Falls

Phyllida	a maker and a Maroon
Doudou Laguerre	a rabble rouser and muse to Zeynab
Mattie	an artisan and doyenne
Tamika	a diseuse and rootworker
Dom	a world-builder and stowaway

The Pitch

In which Zeynab weighs the risk of epistemological violence

ZEYNAB CALLS HERSELF an artist. Teetering at the edge of a precipice, calculating the series of daring maneuvers that will reorganize the terrain around her. Up. Down. Over. Under. And who could imagine all the things she would do for the sake of her craft.

She's hungry. Why else would she sit in a lobby, waiting for an executive assistant to call her into a pitch meeting at the New Stockholm Film Commission. She wants the grant. No, she needs it. Working with a budget, for once, would allow her to finish her project, or, at the very least, silence the static in her head. If only she could stay present long enough to deliver her pitch, which she practiced in the shower, in the mirror, to a drunk stranger at a bar.

Her pitch is solid, if only for the fact that it hinges on her charisma. Otherwise, her methodology is obscure. Her process is vague. Her body is the vehicle. She did, after all, finesse her way into this meeting by way of an audio documentary that spread, first underground in her circles, and then overground in the mainstream circuit, until it reached the institutional shores of the Film Commission. No application forms. No automatic email responses. No waiting around while elastic processing times and rolling deadlines stretch her resources past the point of hope.

For a well-funded government agency, their lobby needs a refresh. From the outside, the brutalist architecture communicates blunt authority. The interior design doubles down on the severity and asks, "What did you expect on a public-sector budget?" She does, however, appreciate the color palette, its soothing blandness. Every surface is draped in varying shades of gray, burgundy touches, speckled with the bit of sunlight that peaks through undersized windows. Even the fluorescents subdue everything to a matte texture. The only sources of variance are the posters of past projects, displayed on the walls in chronological order, in increasingly colorful design, visual proof of the institution's editorial progression.

In this decor, she feels the distance between herself and the bustling street below. She visualizes herself as a dot scurrying on the ground 15 floors down, thoughts drowned out by the commotion of other bottom feeders. Here, she has to strain to detect the hum of the central heating, the rumble of a self-satisfied machine.

She's principled. While she waits, she speculates on what it would mean to sell her project. Because it is indeed a sale. To an institution like this, what is a story but a commodity? By its logic, people, pain, and places are mere inputs. Every spreadsheet in this building translates these inputs to games of shadow and light that generate cultural capital meant to reify the state's legitimacy. Somewhere, a few floors down, digital and material archives swell the coffers and influence the colony's imagination of itself.

Just by entering this lobby, she has opened the possibility of accessing these coffers and depositing an offering. She resents approaching these illegitimate gatekeepers, positioning herself as a native informant to be vetted by a set of government officials who will have the final say in constructing her or other people's story. And yet, she sits there, rehearsing points, tying together her narrative arc, sanding down the edges of nuance, whittling down flesh and blood people into protagonists, into a three-act structure.

For a moment, she allows herself to eavesdrop on the murmur that leaks through the adjacent wall. Somebody's in there, chatting in a relaxed tone, as if to a long-time friend. The content of their speech is indecipherable. At one point, Zeynab thinks she hears the words, "impact production" and "target audience," but she can't be sure. She imagines the team of producers, how they must nod approvingly, hanging onto this person's every word.

When the person exits the room, Zeynab realizes that it's another documentary filmmaker whose work she knows. That their appearance does not match their voice. That there's a look of hunger on their face that asks, "Have I fucked this up? Will I starve on a diet of my own mediocrity?" She knows this face well because it is also her own.

She's glad she went with a crisp white dress shirt, straight-legged trousers, and a solid silk hijab. It's boring as hell, a business-casual rig, but it will make her legible. As for her human anatomy, she was raised to understand that if anyone judges her based on anything intrinsic about her, it is evidence of their own alienation, that they can go fuck themselves.

She is egoless. When she first walked up to reception, the polite-yet-distant executive assistant never squinted and didn't ask if she was lost. Although she did not reciprocate her excessively friendly greeting, she offered her an espresso. Zeynab accepted a cup, even if something told her that one isn't supposed to take the espresso. Then the exec assistant mercifully proceeded to ignore her.

Upon entering the meeting room, she sees that the selection committee is composed of two producers, a lead and an associate. The lead producer, a white man, looms over her and makes insufficient eye contact when he shakes her hand. Mostly harmless. Creased smile. Pink face like smoked ham. Big hands. He seems at a loss for what to do with them. One moment he's fiddling with a pen, clicking the tip in and out, in and out, the next, he smooths a graying patch of hair at his temples. More like the passive recipient of structural advantages than a confident potentate.

The associate producer is his perfect counterpart. Hungry. Razor sharp. Speaks in clipped sentences, like she expects everyone to have read the memo already. They're unfortunate, these optics and division of labour, that of a power-imbalanced married couple. One can imagine her straightening his tie, wiping a crumb from the side of his mouth, topping him from the bottom. And there's a glint in her eye. Behind her facade of professionalism lurks a nugget of contempt. She would be the first to betray him in a coup.

Zeynab has a powerful handshake. She knows well enough to engage the muscles in a way that conveys her trustworthiness. The trick is to focus on transmitting clear intentions. Deploy them in one or two spirited pumps. Easy now. Produce a smile when offered a pleasantry. Don't overdo it. Although it grosses her out, her mouth waters at the prospect of validation.

The New Stockholm Film Commission's mandate is to Bolster, Produce, and Distribute Innovative and Imaginative Audiovisual Works that Reflect the Diverse Realities and Perspectives within the Nation and the Rest of the World.

That's how the lead producer recites the institutional mandate, by capitalizing the first letter of each word, like it's a spell that conjures credibility, as if everyone hasn't read the website.

As he speaks, the associate producer seems checked out. Like she's heard this spiel for the nth time and it's just white noise to her. She snaps back to attention when she catches Zeynab's eyes on her. She returns the look with a phony grin, no eye muscles engaged. Judging by the way the lead producer pauses and defers to her every time he concludes a sentence, it's clear she has the final say in this place.

Zeynab is calculated. When the time comes to describe the project, she inhales deeply and launches into the constellation of incidents that make her documentary not only urgent, but compelling. While speaking, she suppresses her vocal fry and censors the rising inflections at the end of her sentences, like a news anchor. She notices the parts of her rehearsed speech that pique interest, the portions that fall flat.

Early into Zeynab's preamble about New Stockholm's de facto expropriatory urban policy, the associate producer peers at the clock behind her, indicating that she's heard it all before, that her ass should move it along. The producer's attention flits back to her as soon as she mentions her leads. Her entry point into the story includes a handful of activists who break into the sprawling construction site to destroy equipment owned by a defense construction company, redundantly named Defense Construction Incorporated. The very same semi-public corporation that cheerfully proposed to pave over the neighbourhood of Cipher Falls.

Now she has their attention. That's when she lays it on even thicker, asserts her privileged access to the story, and suggests that, yes sure, some white-guy filmmaker could try to tackle the same subject, just storm in there with his beard-sporting director of photography and crotch-scratching sound recordist, but that what she offers is an intimate angle, a singular point of view that would demonstrate to the public, their constituents, the Diverse aspect of their mandate.

Immediately, after she says it, she can tell that this was apparently a gauche thing to say, that it landed on ears that aren't used to hearing this discourse, tepid as it is. The lead producer seems at a loss with what to make of it, and has already deferred to the associate producer for a reaction.

Zeynab's depersonalized. From the opposite corner of the meeting room, she perceives herself, that awkward, slightly pleading posture in the office chair, how she holds her espresso, ankles crossed against each other in that protective way that comes to her when she's anxious.

The past always seems layered onto the present. She sees herself sitting in the dining room of a familiar low-rise apartment that faces a parking lot. It always looks smaller and more run-down than she remembers.

She's candid. The child of political asylum seekers, she strategically discloses her personal history, namely, the adjacent social housing project into which she was born and raised, now a dog park. Its cultural importance. Its swift dismantling. The political climate that foretells the potential demise of Cipher Falls.

She evokes her late father, at his usual spot at the dining room table. How spry and energetic he was, though initially he showed no signs of the sickness that would detonate in his body. Her father's face, that would come to exist as a palimpsest, memories layered over features. For a while, as his illness progressed, her life would become entwined in his caregiving. She would never forget the pulse of his becoming and unbecoming—not that he was diminished but concentrated to his essential self—when he would spend his days in bed, eyes closed, hooked up to a respiratory machine, where his breathing, metered in khrr khrrs, would cadence the end of his life.

And, of course, she recalls her mother. Mainly her absence, but also her traces. How she was the textile that generated the pattern of their lives, from the placement of the couch in the living room, to the color of the walls, a burnished orange that evokes the sunsets of her childhood. She would miss the atmosphere of driving down a stretch of highway. How carefree she seemed when she placed a bare foot on the dashboard, wiggling her toes to the music. Gone too soon, she would leave behind this fragile material archive as well as an ineffable inheritance. The way a word is whispered. A proclivity for hot drinks and unanswerable questions. A combative posture that paved the way for Zeynab's independence of expression.

The longer she sits in the producers' office expounding on the intangible, the more she becomes shaken, flayed, contorted in that awkward posture. There is now a coffee stain on her sleeve, and the atmosphere around her has thickened. The lead and associate producers both lean into her.

"Well," the lead clears his throat, "that's interesting."

She holds her breath.

He strokes his chin and looks to his colleague who rubs her temples, as if to massage away the sting of a thought.

And then, to her surprise, the associate asks, "Tell us, Zeynab. When, exactly, would you be ready to start production?"

As they stand up and extend their hands, she stares back at them and finally exhales. She is flabbergasted, but regains her composure and returns their handshakes. And just like that, the whole business of the pitch is over.

"This month," she declares, without skipping a beat. It's an overestimation, a timeline she's not sure how she would even manage to achieve. With her mind still hovering over the memory of her parents, she hears herself reiterate, "I can start this month."

She's an artist, and will fill in those details along the way.

you can touch, but it'll cost you

In which Phyllida's motive is clear,
despite the implausible method

I HATE FRY DUTY. No matter how gingerly I lower the basket into the deep fryer, the hot oil lashes out at me. During today's shift, I leave a batch in for so long that it smokes and sets off the kitchen alarm, which sounds like a human scream. I jump out of my skin, and there is a horrible splash. Seconds later, blisters crop up on my forearm. It would have been worse had I not run to the sink right away, made tracks over Maria's fresh mop job, which she cussed me out for spoiling.

Ted, our manager, says I should look into workers' comp. But, get this, the fucking way he says it. Just when I have my arm submerged under cold running water and everybody is freaking out about backed-up fry orders, he squeezes right behind me and rubs his knob on my hip, leaving a scent trail of Nautica Voyage and unwashed uniform, making out like he was reaching for a rag from the sink, except that he wasn't.

"Nah, yeah, Phyllida," he says. "See, that's definitely a first-degree burn, almost a second."

"Oh?"

Seemingly accidentally, I sink an elbow into his lower rib/ upper gut.

"Ouch. Yeah, the manual says we only cover second-degree burns and upwards."

"Oh."

Too bad. I could have used the payout to subsidize my next tattoo, maybe get the fuck out of this dump, away from this perv.

For what it's worth, the scarring on my arm is glorious. From the back of my hand to the crook of my elbow, the discolored tissue against melanin gives me a stretch of polka-dot skin. Stripped of its deep color to a sickly pink, the scalded area reminds me of novelty leather goods, like crocodile hide. As I apply Polysporin along my arm, I count seventeen blisters of varying sizes, from the circumference of a ladybug to the contour of a dime.

Later that week, on a bus ride home from work, I contemplate the swollen marks with such fervor that I miss my stop. The walk isn't necessarily lengthy, but it's a bit of a maze, weaving through the roped-off craters in the ground that mark where they want to implant a concrete behemoth in the middle of the neighbourhood. Just a couple of blocks from my apartment, a pylon materializes out of nowhere and trips me, such that I graze my forearms against hot asphalt, aggravating the flesh bubbles. I have no choice but to prick them one by one and watch the fluid ooze, wondering what it tastes like. Probably well water.

Three days later, once the burn turns to crust, I accentuate my arm with two cuff leather bracelets and a formidable cheetah print vest with cut-off sleeves. I draw looks everywhere I go.

Reactions are nonstop when I'm assigned to the cash register. The arm has a magnetic force. The most jaded customers stop in their tracks while placing their orders and gawk at my forearm. Some eye me with sympathy. Most seem grossed out.

Now I only need to raise an eyebrow when some dissociated asshole is hemming and hawing "Uhhhh, lemme get a..." about whether they should upsize to combo no. 6 or go in on a double chocolate fudge sundae. Not even cut eye, just a bit of resting bitch face, and they immediately retreat.

"Never mind, I'll just take a medium."

The only client who protests openly is a mother with an antsy toddler perched on her hip, who wants a small strawberry shake.

"Should you be serving people in that condition?" She asks, wrinkling her nose at me and shifting the baby higher on her hip. "Seems unsanitary."

"So just the milkshake then?"

At the very mention, the toddler wiggles even more.

"Millshae!"

She pauses, and eyes me suspiciously, before nodding.

"Debit, credit, cash?"

"Cash."

She flings a five-dollar bill on the counter, as if in fear of my touch.

*

Tamika notices the arm as soon as I walk into her tattoo studio.

"Oh bèbi, what happened?"

"Workplace injury."

She rolls her eyes. Not at me. The Dunbar. Where people go to get ritually food poisoned.

"I can't wait for you to leave that place behind."

"You and me both."

"Did you see that full moon last night?"

"Like a wheel of Parmigiano."

"Like an ovarian cyst."

"Like a ripe pomelo."

"Like a–"

Her eyes dart to a point behind me and suddenly her face hardens.

Some dude looms inside the doorway, which I could have sworn I'd locked.

"Hey, do you do tribal pieces?" he says.

"I don't do walk-ins."

"Oh? Well, alright. I'll just have a look around."

"Actually, you'll just have to get the hell out."

Briefly, he pauses and considers whether he does, in fact, have to get the hell out. You can only tell when observing Tamika from the side, but she has hyperkyphosis that curves her back forward. When she's facing you, standing at full height, she seems poised to pounce on your throat or kiss you. Depends on the dynamic. As we stare him down, his eyes flit from her face to mine. We breathe into the occasion and wonder if this is going to turn into a showdown. After seven excruciating seconds, he steps backward and out the door, looking like he was just forced to eat a shit sandwich. Tamika immediately rushes over and twists the lock closed.

"Fucking marauders. Would saunter right up my pussy if they could."

Her station: an empty storefront in the abandoned outlet mall, which she gussied up with fairy lights and macramé wall hangings. In the far corner, a bassinet containing Bijou, who sleeps with a wry face, wee fists balled up inside their no-scratch mittens. While Tamika preps the equipment, I inch my face close to Bijou's to see if they might wake up and grace me with their attention. No such luck. Their eyelids remain sealed to my big anxious face. So I hang back and check out the prints stuck to the wall. Between the gangling salamanders and hippocampuses, there's a handsome-looking Ouroboros, the namesake of Tamika's collective. She knows how to take the tail and feed it back to the hungry beast.

Five minutes into lying on the table with my chest exposed, fear grips my body, makes me the little spoon. I tolerate needles, but there's something about a continuous poke that scares the shit out of me. Reason why I hate penetration.

There's the smell of rubbing alcohol and latex gloves while she disinfects the area. Despite my outward layer of cool, my insides feel quiet and vaporous. I smoked a joint before coming in and popped a couple of aspirin codeine pills left over from my mother's hysterectomy.

"You sure you don't wanna wait for this to heal?" she asks, looking at my forearms.

"Nah, I'm good. It's old news," I try to reassure her.

"Phyllida, girl. If you need time, we can always push this session back to an optimal date."

Ever so cautious, that's why I love her, want her to place her indelible mark on me.

Using a flimsy disposable razor, she starts shaving my belly, working her way upward in a linear motion, in measured strokes. The friction generates a kind of heat under my skin. Mere gestures away from lovemaking. My chest has barely a coating of peach fuzz, but Tamika's working at it meticulously. I can taste the metal of the blade.

When Tamika makes her way to my ribcage, it tingles so much that I squirm.

"Hihihi, that's—"

"Shhh. Don't want to nick you," she mumbles through her teeth.

And then she follows up with a cooling swipe of rubbing alcohol.

She hums an unidentifiable tune while working. Her thick-lensed glasses give her an air of intense focus, which only adds to her charm. Tamika is a prophetess and prayer warrior. She has a gift. Regression therapy revealed to her that someone in her maternal lineage drew veves by spilling cornmeal before ceremonies. No wonder she's obsessed with fine lines and symbolism. She seems born to draw oracles and would have been celebrated for her powers had she designed the city herself.

And then it starts. Huddled above me, illuminated by the studio's magnifying LED lamp, she's a feast for the eyes. Her gash-red lipstick has faded so that what's left are precise strokes of lip liner around her sour tobacco-smelling mouth. She looks like a fabulously inked surgeon. Better yet, her intricate eye makeup and facial piercings recall a warrior mask. I try my best to stay still, but I feel an untimely fit of laughter working its way through me, threatening to explode if I hold it in any longer.

"Just a minute." I hold up a hand.

She pauses and frowns.

"You sure you've got this?"

Her mood has shifted from her usual gracious customer service persona from when we'd planned the tattoo to the officious demeanor of a contractor. "*Sorry ma'am, what you have here is structural.*"

The codeine aspirin is kicking in. I can tell because my breathing has slowed, like I'm about to pass out.

“No, yeah, go ahead.”

She squints at me for a few seconds more. I struggle to invert my smile and deliver my most sober mug. Something about the act of suppressing a smile has an unintended effect. A sudden ripple of sadness overtakes me.

I’m scared that she will send me away. To my relief, she sighs and turns the machine on again.

The outline is coming along. The sketch is top-notch, but I can’t wait to see it on my skin. Months ago, I’d booked this piece on my solar plexus. The tattoo in question: A siren that came to me in a dream. I can’t draw for shit. But, all from memory, I was able to relay her precise vibe, sunken eyes, pointed breasts, not to mention the coiling braids that slunk down around her like algae, except for a few tendrils that entangled a disproportionately small ship in its clutches.

Not sure where I’ve seen her before. I guess she’s the fruit of my subconscious. Those eyes and their slow blink. They’ve been seared into my brain since that dream.

When I described her, Tamika picked up on her immediately. Hella clairvoyant. I wasn’t even two sentences in, and she’d already shaded in the details.

“Mind if I put on something?”

“Not at all.”

"What do you feel like?"

"Um, let's see. Neurostep. Speedcore. Acid Trance... Anything in that musical neighbourhood, really."'

"Got it."

We end up listening to a noise album on repeat. *Subterrane*, a collection of field recordings produced by a local artist who hooked up a controller to an abandoned house in Old Cipher Falls and extracted the creaking, thrumming, rumbling sonic matter from the structure. House sounds amplified. It works out well because it covers the sound of my grumbling stomach. Should've eaten.

The tattoo session is like grief itself. Raw. Messy. Phobic.

We're talking critical levels of pain. Like when I visited my mother in the recovery room after her surgery and she was too groggy to return my hug yet lucid enough to ask why I was dressed like such a hussy.

Electromagnetic surges that last way too long. I don't know if I can manage this much sensation. So much consciousness forced out of me at once, threatening to blow out of my ears, nose, and other holes. Tears will do for now.

Bitch of a session. We stop and start three more times. The first, so that I can order dumplings from a place across the street. The second, so that I can smoke a little roach. The third, so that Tamika can nurse Bijou.

She congratulates me when I slide off her table five hours later.

"You did well. Didn't know you had it in you."

"Thanks."

I scratch my head, unsure of what to do next. The codeine aspirin has faded into a dull headache. I'm standing in the middle of the studio, topless. I feel lightheaded and unmoored, in need of a hug. As soon as I step toward her, arms outstretched, she grabs ahold of my hand.

"Easy there. Have a seat."

I slide back onto the tattoo table.

"How are you feeling?"

I shrug.

"Would you like to be sung to?"

I shrug again.

Tamika wraps her arms around me and rocks me gently while singing that same tune. This time with lyrics.

Wander with the herd.
Play under the sun.
Splash in the lagoon.

You chase your tail, baby elephant.
But did you know you can also go to sleep?

I ride a taxi home that evening. Sprawled out on the backseat, I grumble curt answers in response to the driver as he pretends to make conversation, fishing around for my marital status.

As soon as I reach my apartment, I pop another two codeine aspirins. There's no more weed in my tin, so I grind dried lavender, roll it, and light a joint on my balcony. Heady stuff.

As usual, my roommate Dom is immersed in their games in the dimmed living room, bathed in the glow of their laptop. Floating head.

On the kitchen counter, a tall stack of clean bowls awaits me, a passive aggressive sculptural installation. I grab one and fill it with fresh grapes, blowing a kiss at Dom as I pass them again in the living room. They nod back.

Right before bed, the business of peeling off my shirt is painstaking.

I rest on top of my bedspread and lie on my back like a starfish. A spider on my ceiling spies on me, occasionally rubbing its front legs together, like it's plotting a journey into my hot cavern of a mouth.

For the most part, I sleep through the night, except for when I wake up around 3am and realize that I've rolled onto my stomach. To my horror, the whole weight of my topless chest is pressed against the tat. I run immediately to the bathroom and assess the damage.

As I rinse off goo and crust, granted, much earlier than the advised twenty-four hours, I catch sight of my burn scars, or rather, the lack thereof. The people at Polysporin must have revamped their formula because the marks have nearly disappeared. More like watercolor strokes than the angry etchings they once were. And then there's the mermaid's face. Her expression is fiercer than I remember, but I chalk it up to the swollen skin that tugs at the lines that Tamika meticulously poked at the studio.

"You know what tells me how a face will turn out?" she'd said.

"Nah, what?"

"Eyes. The way they hold secrets. I never know how a face will turn out until I do the eyes."

*

The first thing I do in the morning is clean and dry the tattoo. The siren's expression has mellowed in the light of day.

My mouth is pasty and my head is clouded. All I want to do is wake and bake, maybe work on the beaded piece

I'd started a week ago. I'm not sure where I'm going with it. To those who ask, I say I'm completing pieces for my line. But these hours of shifting and squinting don't seem to amount to much. And I always get the sense that I'm behind on something urgent.

I text Frantz, my sometimes-dealer, to meet me in front of our usual spot. I don't bother checking his response, just head there an hour later, and he's waiting for me, holding a bouquet of grocery-store carnations. What a guy. One whose horniness arises from a deep sense of veneration. In fine form as usual, he greets me by gawking at my ass. I pretend not to notice that he looks like he wants to tear my bodice apart and ravish me right there on this grassy hill, which reminds me of the big sad back of a marooned humpback whale. As soon as we sit, he reaches for my foot. I kick his hand away.

I like that Frantz will drive 45 minutes from the suburbs just to eat my ass. How hungry he is for it. I appreciate that he does his own housekeeping. Doesn't even wait for me to offer him a glass of water when he walks through the door. He just reaches for a mason jar and pours himself some tap water. Once he grabbed the one we fill with soapy water and grubby sponges to wash the dishes. I don't think he minded, judging from the way he guzzled it in one bolt.

We eventually lie back on the grassy hill, right on the whale's dorsal fin, and watch the clouds roll by while he rolls me a series of joints and catches me up on the latest. "You see that crabapple tree over there?"

"Yeah."

"She's cranky because an old sewer line is blocking her roots."

"You don't say."

"Yeah. But she's working through it."

"Good for her."

"Aw come on, Phyllie–"

"–So, what's the rarified edge of New Stockholm like?"

"You know. Just burbs. Streets named after the trees they chopped down. Are you gonna visit?"

"You gonna hold me captive in your condo?"

"Just might."

"..."

"Might look into a plot of land too sometime."

"What for?"

"Growing a little something."

"Yeah?"

"I'd definitely plant some crabapples. Raise the tone of the place."

"No doubt."

The afternoon spirals away on that hill, while we smoke and talk shit, until the sun blazes red, claims my attention, then ducks away beneath the skyline.

I drift home that evening, on the back of a dragon's tail. Breathing in the smell of baked concrete, I thank myself for taking the rest of the week off to give myself time to heal. Good thing I'd saved up some coin, cause I don't know how I would have handled full shifts. I can barely use that arm. Knowing Ted, he would've probably put me on fries again. Cold bastard.

*

On my first day back at work, it feels like a spell is broken. I go slow. My chest burns and my uniform shirt chafes against it.

And then there's Ted. For the first part of the shift, he leaves me alone, but then, as soon as the rush dies down, he closes in on me. As I reach for a fry basket, he grasps my upper arm, and just so happens to graze my titty meat. I look into his face for signs of premeditation and all I see is an eyebrow ring, mocking eyes, and the air of a man who refuses to be seen in his corruption. At that moment, it feels like my titty meat becomes the Dunbar's titty meat. He might as well pluck it off me and throw it on the grill. He leans in and his greasy mouth is so close to mine that I can smell the pickles from the burger he scarfed during his break.

"Hey, tough guy. How's all that scar tissue coming along?"

The oil vat. So shiny and potent. In that golden brown rectangle, I see a vision of the past, present, and future, coiled into one, each thread looping into the next. This vision reveals a premonition of what Ted would want: me, bearing his children, working side by side at the Dunbar, smelling of fries together, our little ones eating from the kids' menu, chicken nuggets and neon orange drink.

I see that future for what it is: my face, ass, voice transposed onto whatever shape stands before Ted, domination-ready, disposable, fuckable, a long line of wifey-offering vessels in front of which I just happen to be standing.

What forces shaped him this way? Is it an unformed substance that's activated by certain elements, like the waxy butter-yellow chunks that we heat against the heating elements?

And who decides whose power gets activated when? See Maria, and her ever-meticulous mop jobs. At what point might she snap that wooden handle in half and drive the splintered end into Ted's heart? Instead of cowering behind her bucket, pretending he doesn't also reach for her booty when he gets the chance. Or could the sludgy water streaks on the floor gain sentience and collude to collect underfoot as Ted makes his way past me, reducing the grinding of his knob on my hip, the grasping at my titty meat, the friction between his rubber soles and the floor, launching him downward and backward with a good crack to the head?

And who can say what possessed Ted to plunge his own face into the oil vat? In the middle of peak hours, such as the ones we work, temperatures shoot up to 375 degrees Fahrenheit, enough to gelatinize starches and render crispy skin on carb or flesh.

They say it was a third-degree burn. Don't know if he got worker's comp though.

Box Braid

In which Mattie's rheumatism flares up

CORNROWS FOR 250. Box braids for 370. Another 120 for a wash and press. No perm. No dye. This is what I tell the girl in the silk head wrap when she walks through my door.

In response, her brow pops up in indignation like I just reached for her intimate centre, but I pay her no mind. My face closes off to her. When the clientele sees me soften, that's when the wheedling and needling starts, as do complicated requests for Sisterlocks or Bantu Knots, and I don't need the botheration.

Eileen jokes that my face is as expressive as a mackerel's, all downturned brow and frown lines. I chalk it up to fifteen years of living in this city of beggars and scammers. Let me tell you what I do: whatever I can to avoid it. It chips away at you, the business of making your way in the world, skating from one appointment to the next, climbing stairs, descending them, pulling doors, pushing them, bumping up against people, pushing past them. Impossible to mobilize your facial muscles to please when they are bound so tightly to your heart by a tendon that channels each worry and trifle.

Silk Head Wrap Girl stands in my hallway like a trapped mouse, like I'm about to nyam her. As if there's any meat on those bones. I ask if she ate. She shakes her head, no. So I leave her there and shuffle to the kitchen and fix her a foaming glass of Milo and a plateful of glucose biscuits.

When I come back to the hallway, she's still standing where I left her, but has finally removed her jacket. She hands me a bag of hair. I hand her the glass and plate. No thank you, she motions. I chups and say, take it. She takes it.

As we move to the living room, I see how her eyes flit about, scanning my yucca, ficus, and areca palms for signs of danger. Trust, if there's a menace, it comes from beyond these walls. The excreta-borne pathogens that coat every surface of the subway. My mendacious landlord. The white neighbour who shouts at his girlfriend when he's not playing video games.

That's why I only take referrals. People are in cruel form these days. All you have to do is observe them long enough, watch for the signs, and sure enough, they'll try to exploit you, unless you catch them first.

That's why I work my magic from home.

I paid a heavy price the last time I spent a day outside. Back when I made house calls. I rendezvoused with a man with a Jheri curl at the Dunbar place that sells some semblance of food. He sold me a hairdresser trolley at a competitive price, I thought.

That trolley, I pushed it back to Montego Place, congratulating myself for the solid deal, brainstorming how I would organize my supplies into its many compartments.

I was fetching a box of beef patties from the freezer in the narrowest aisle when I caught sight of Jheri Curl again. How intimately we locked eyes. All while holding my gaze, he snatched the trolley which I'd abandoned for nary a moment. Mercy. Before I could gesture or shout, he had ducked and woven his way out of the store. By then, I could only push my way back to the empty spot he'd left.

Should've known better. When I'd handed him cash for the case, he'd eyed me like a dog on a steak, curling his lips back into a snarl that disappeared his whole smile into his gums. In retrospect, it was clear that he was bridling unspeakable motives. His handshake was the sweatiest palm stroke I've ever felt. You can't Purell away that kind of physical memory.

Could've been worse. If I hadn't made that stop at the market, the ragamuffin might have followed me home and had his way with me. Or was he still on the hunt? This fear tormented me on the two-kilometre walk that coils around those vexatious infrastructure projects and sprawls into a 40-minute walk under frigid rain on the precipice of winter. No wallet. No phone. Not even a cough drop to my name. I'd left my purse in the trolley. Just chafed thighs from walking that distance. At least the woman at the counter let me buy a patty on credit, which I ate on the road to warm up. Those patties are choke-dry. I walked under a rainstorm, getting more drenched by the minute, as if the Lord himself wept tears of laughter on my head.

*

I take a seat in the living room and throw a cushion between my legs. I direct Silk Head Wrap Girl to the designated seat. As soon as her bottom lands in front of me, I grab for the remote and turn on the TV.

She smells of streets. A mixture of hot asphalt and construction dust clinging to adrenal secretions, as if she ran for the bus, gave up, then legged it again. My nose gets it right every time. I spend most of my days in this controlled environment. I know how every inch of the apartment smells, from the unripeness of my stunted flowering trees to the rot of a forgotten sponge behind the sink. Most of all, my own smell envelops me. I bathe every day in essential oils, milk and salt. No deodorant necessary. My natural scent is that of a ripe papaya.

We flip to the vintage cartoon channel. Babar is on. What felt so cheery as a child now makes me grimace. Don't be fooled by procedural dramas, not even the rape kind. It's the children's programmes that air the most brutality. Vehicles for encoded violence. My father never let me watch Tintin, that fascist little cop. Nor Babar and its colonized elephants and indomitable rhinos in suits placed at odds in a banana republic. Note the trifling white woman in their midst. The heavy-handedness of it all.

Sure enough, Silk Head Wrap Girl is already transfixed by the idiot box. I watch her watch it. Mouth agape, shoulders slumped, she crunches the biscuits and soaks them in gulps of Milo, like she's unused to eating in the company of others. I almost regret offering her refreshments.

People have no housetraining. My former subletter drank from juice cartons while letting the refrigerator door dangle open every morning. I've never erased the sight of his Adam's apple, the way it bobbed up and down, spoiling my view of sunrise. My senses are damn near triggered watching from above as Silk Head Wrap's temples work furiously. I turn up the volume and focus on Babar as he walks the gardens with the white lady, worrying about rhino shenanigans. I wonder how the elephant queen feels about their emotional affair.

Then we get going. Unceremoniously, without peeling her eyes away from the screen, she folds the headwrap, several meters of galaxy-patterned fabric that she lays on her knees in a neat pile. Smoothing it with her palm, she suddenly relaxes her shoulders.

The money's not necessarily in braids. But I'm one of the few who can make a living from a steady base of clients. Put me in a lineup with other hairdressers and I'd probably be the last one these girls recognize. Sometimes, I run into them at the grocery store, the subway, the pharmacy. They stare past me. I reckon they only recognize the touch of my fingers.

But I don't take just anybody. My trick is to test the integrity of each prospective client. Hush-hush, I'll slip them a few extra bills with their change when they hand me my payment. I don't return calls from those who don't immediately correct me. Saves me revenue in the long run.

I've been perfecting my technique. For this reason, I think most of them are surprised at my manner, when they see the apparent cheerfulness of my hair designs. Don't be fooled by my elegant plaits. Only the most discerning can see through the hot-oil treatments and edge control and understand what I'm trying to create.

Another upside is that I can work in my panties. Crank the thermostat to the max, and you'd mistake this place for a Jacmel beach on a Saturday afternoon, complete with grilling smells. My window faces a fast food joint that uses copious amounts of garlic which travels through the alleyway and seeps through the slits of my bedroom window and leaves me with the distinct impression that someone's in my kitchen. But I wouldn't eat there again unless I wanted to spend the better part of an afternoon breathing and burping garlic, leaking salty tears from heartburn. Sometimes the teenagers who work there come out to smoke and talk nonsense about the boss and the noisy deliveries that come through every Monday and Wednesday.

Can you crack a window, she asks. I shake my head, no. Trust these daft clients to come here and disrupt my ecosystem. If I let the temperature fall too low, my babies won't survive it. Not a week ago, the hydrangea almost wilted beyond repair. Most of my utility expenses go toward heating this place, maintaining a steady regime of photosynthesis with the grow lights.

She frowns. Sweat beads glisten on her forehead. Chups. I put down the comb, go to the kitchen, and come back with a Diet Coke. She gulps it down fast and loud, nearly drowning herself in the substance.

The moment I get started, I can already feel my hands jam up. It starts in the balls of my wrist and travels to the second, major, and first knuckles of my right hand. By the time this session is over, they will swell up like boiled okra.

I rifle through the bundles of hair. 100% Kanekalon. Three packs of 1B-Off Black and a pack of Ombré Turquoise. While I unwrap it, she fidgets in her seat, asks for the mirror. Doubting Thomas. She seems to be one of those fanciful girls who want to hear all this palaver about hairstyling school this, certificate that, glossy magazines in the waiting room, cucumber water while you wait.

I don't do all that.

*

Eileen says a certification would make me competitive on the market. She says, Mattie, why don't you invest in yourself?

It's not that I didn't try. Another cursed day I spent outside.

Bad omen: I sneezed five times in a row as soon as I entered the Cipher Falls Community Centre conference room. No windows. Jailhouse slats, the kind that screech with rust when you try to wind them open. Father god, the building is cursed. Rumor has it that this is where the police used to illegally interrogate the youths. No doubt, it still holds a whiff of fear, youthful naiveté, and confusion. My eyes watered and clouded when I first looked at the room, its chairs and desks, which were composed of plastic and wood veneer, a frozen-in-time office catalog from the 70s. Made my skin crawl. I'm sensitive to textures. Thank goodness I'd brought a shawl.

The instructor, a representative of the New Stockholm Employment and Social Service Centre, had the demeanor of a youth pastor, all smiles and crinkly eyes. He started off by sermonizing.

"Do you know why each of you is here today?"

He paused for effect.

> "It's not just because we want to play gatekeeper to the New Stockholm hairstyling and aesthetics industry. It's not because you have nothing better to do on a Saturday morning."

As he spoke, he manifested a nervous tic of sniffling abruptly, as if he suffered from allergies.

> "It's not because we might get to take credit for your success somewhere down the line, although we don't discount any of those reasons. I mean, this is the real world, folks. You've gotta bring your authentic self wherever you go. Perhaps even your cultural background! But fundamentally, it's because we value the gifts that each of you bring to the table."

When he said "table," he rapped on his desk, which, had it been made of solid wood, like acacia or a nice teak, would have added the gravitas I believe he was looking for. Instead, all we heard were empty slaps. How embarrassed I was for him.

> "I truly, and I mean, truly, believe that there's something about each of you that is special and that you deserve to become well-rounded hairstylists who are confident behind the chair. We don't even know what jobs will be like in 10 to 15 years. Because the form and nature of jobs is changing so quickly, it's difficult to know where training like this will lead. The final frontier is very vague."

And then he produced what one might call a smile, if hard-pressed.

> "But ultimately, we are very optimistic that people like you represent the future. Especially given the fact

> that birth and death rates are the way they are. We must lean into this attrition rate."

At the end of his monologue, there was a ten-second lag during which he smiled earnestly. Dead silence. I looked around the room to confirm that everyone else was still alive and well. And then there was a slow clap that emanated from one corner of the room, which amplified into a rain of applause among the others. The instructor looked so radiant, like a spinster on her wedding day. His tic intensified so much that I rifled through my purse to see if I could find him a Clarinex.

But then, a demonstration of another order came from an official from the provincial Ministry of Training and Labour, who showed up from who knows where to entreat us with a personal greeting, if you can call it that. A carceral touch, if you will. While she did so, the instructor did a roll call and distributed fat little folders that contained a fact sheet, a branded notebook, and a programme that we were to consult daily to abide by the schedule. And then she was gone.

Imagine my surprise, on that first day of the training, when I unpacked all my good combs, just as the others unsheathed their laptop computers.

Rather than doing hair, we watched a computer presentation on how to do hair.

It felt like the longest period I'd ever sat for anything, and I've done micro-braids on a big-headed girl. On the way to class that morning, I made the mistake of buying coffee from that greasy Dunbar place across the street. From the acidity of the brew, I could tell that it wouldn't bode well for my irritable bowels. I made sure to visit the restroom before the last half of the session. Next thing, I'm crouching in a stall over a bowl to keep my trembling thighs from brushing the seat.

I washed my hands so zealously that the industrial soap in the washroom, that harsh pink almond oil, aggravated my eczema.

There's no denying it. I'm the most fragile of birds.

Needless to say, that was my last day of that. I just ignored Eileen the next time she asked me how school was going.

*

I've known too many brave ones who rushed out into the world and into the arms of demons. They come to me broken, destroyed, hanging by a literal thread.

This one is no different. The moment she unwraps her hair, I see it for what it is.

Damaged terrain. The scalp itself is raised and itchy. At her crown lies a map of trials and tribulations. I've seen my share of strained roots, frayed edges, split strands in the crowns of neglected clients, but nothing to this extent. If there's something these arthritic fingers know, she's in danger.

I barely touch her head but she bristles at my fingertip. I lighten my touch. She relaxes again into the TV programme. Damned near lost in it. I take another close look at the scalp, its fine grain of open pores pulled by tight strands, as if she or someone else had taken to yanking at her like a rag doll, as a mother would nip a cat by the nape, and in other spots, like it had suffered continuous rasp of a fingernail.

It's a crooked reflection of everything I don't have.

Ambition. A driving force and vicious streak. A pattern of late nights and bewilderment and a dangling carrot of validation. Eating at her edges.

Expectations. A string of them. Picking away at her life. Guilt, vanity, and bad behaviour. Tearing away at her vitality. Sucking her marrow like so many lampreys, without the slightest ounce of gratitude.

Connection. The want and pursuit of it. Its potential loss and the heartaches that come with it.

My day starts like this: At first light, within the folds of my blankets, I hold my head in both hands and request all the wisdom, blessings, and protection that I can. Then, after I've had a long soak in the tub and performed my weekly exfoliation, followed by a meticulous application of whipped shea butter, I place a blessing on my altar: A piece of chocolate, a sprig of herbs, a splash of rum. You're only just a moment away from slipping into devastation.

For this client, there is hope. A nodule of strength sits on her crown. The same grain that a grandmother or great-grandmother surely had.

While rinsing her head under the sink, I flood the area with compassion. It's no easy task. A film of gunked harm clings to her like an armor. For a time, she even repels moisture. The water just beads into droplets that bounce off her shoulders and onto my bathroom floor. She stands there in her bra, most of it padded in the front. The top of her chest is almost concave, like lunch meats stacked on a platter.

Eventually, my work with the water penetrates the hair shaft and whips up into a thick mangosteen-scented lather. I use extracts from a shipment at Montego Bays. Bless them.

By the time I towel dry her hair, it feels like a new dawn. A favourable path awaits us.

Then I take to the wide-toothed comb.

The first hour is hell. She tenses to my touch and yanks her hypersensitive head away. My back is in tatters. Feels like my spine was ripped up and out by eagle talons. The nerves feel frayed. My fingers lock up the moment that I attempt an ambitious knot. I immediately release the strand of hair. We wince our way through it.

By the third hour, she submits to my knotting, bends in the odd angles that I place her head in search of a better hold. As we progress, my fingers constrict into what feels like a tight fist. In response to my grip, she leans into the pressure, momentarily forgetting herself until I shake her back into position.

This is what I do: I round up all the ambient blessings that I can and trace them into a pattern of faith and loving-kindness. I weave a prayer into each of the strands, from the roots to the tips.

By the fifth hour, we slump into a trance as I braid the Kanekalon into tight cords. As I fall into a triple meter, and a one-and-ah-two-and-ah-three-and-ah rhythm that lulls both our eyes shut. When I open mine again, I find that I'm still braiding. She's watching the Jetsons on TV.

In the sixth and final hour, I lead her by the shoulder to my bathroom, remove the succession of panties left to drip dry on the shower rod and angle her over the tub. She perches on the edge while I pour scalding water from a kettle to seal the braid tips.

After I sponge the excess water, she gets up and beholds herself in the mirror. One moment, she slouches, shivering with goosebumps on her neck. Next, she raises her back straighter.

Trust, she's no prettier than before we started. Her beauty does not come from her hair. She just seems clearer, stronger. The braids wrap around her shoulders, a protective cloak.

Finally, the time comes for her to tuck her hair back in that silk headwrap. She hands me my money in the form of a big bill. I slip a little extra in with the difference. I watch as she rifles through the cash, hesitates a moment, and closes her little fist around the wad. Chups. Just like that, I mentally strike her from my books. But then, moments later, when I escort her to the hallway, she stops, turns and hands me the surplus. Hmm. A welcome surprise, but I'm still perturbed by the initial shilly-shallying. After triple-locking the door, I bend over and snatch the wisps of Kanekalon on the living room floor. Already, I'm thinking of how, tonight, I will soothe my fingers in a steaming bowl of Epsom salt solution and rub them down with Tiger Balm. For now, I pretend not to smile from a job well done.

Ekphrasis I: The Siren

In which Tamika prays

if but some vengeful god would call to me
from the sky, and laugh,
'thou suffering thing,'
know that thy sorrow is my ecstasy,
that thy love's loss is my hate's profiting,

then i would climb up there and snatch him by his low-hanging fruit and bid him never to address me again with that dirty sky mouth unless it's to bless me and make my booty and bank account fatter.

i would call on the daemonic earth entities, our mothers who art underground, to pause their festivities, to hush for a moment, and crack their portal open, for but a fleeting second so that me and my kinfolk and skinfolk may join them for a second.

and following three days and three nights of orgying and feasting and drumming, that we may gather and deliberate on the state of the worlds, the sky, earth, and ether, that have separated like water and oil, such that an alarming number of people have learned to sway to a beat with their hips while their spirits travel to the grocery store and ruminate under its fluorescents the comparative costs of two boxes of cookies, making a choice along the lines of its caloric content, rather than the richness of its mouthfeel and the volume of the involuntary moan that escapes their lips while eating said cookie barefoot in the kitchen at midnight. may they experience a reintegration and healing of these parts.

come tramp stamp or half sleeve, may her call ring clear, that she may sail from rib to rib, across nipple piercing to mole on the collarbone. may she remain vigilant. having contracted and contorted herself, fallen prey to vanity fair, and the encampments of men, having become foam on the wave.

one may try. one may very well try. to be seen. to be heard. to break the water's surface and leave behind all those you knew and cherished. to bend matter and light and shadow, channeling all the elements in such a way that they sing for you, sing a mournful song. oh entities. i pray that we also learn to soften every part of ourselves, let the wrists go limp, let the belly drop, slacken like infants left to fend for themselves on reed boats, rocking in trees. trusting that the wind, the waves, the rolling soil will carry the babe where she needs to go. that she will fatten and grow in due time as the mango tree grows heavy and bears fruit, bending a branch heavy with ripe fruit, and lend a hand to the continuation of the sacred cycle, pass through the system, ever tunneling, emerging on the other side as soil, trusting the seed fragments to sprout anew and give back tenfold.

and earthly daemonic entities, may they pay for their iniquities, not in gold or cowrie shells or legal tender, but through intergenerational curses traveling up and down their lineage, a revolving door of reparations. o earthly mothers–not that i need to ask or pour any more energy, sweat, or tears into the fate of our perpetrators, but may my words seal an already done deal, so to speak, may my voice rise like the song of cicadas over a lush summer pasture, mere soundtrack to a richly furnished decor.

may the homes that they build, on sand, blood, exploitation, creak and groan under the gravity of their sins until cracks and fissures appear and all that is left standing become a haunting reminder of what happens when you fuck with the land, try to grope her with your greedy fingers, fashion her into vain monuments to what you call power. may those pillars, tall as they've erected them, topple down over them and theirs.

The Documentary

In which our intrepid documentarian meets a hotep

As usual, Zeynab had packed a gear case, which contained, among other items, a Bolex camera, a roll of electrical tape, and a Zoom H6 recorder, a clunky device that always drew attention to itself.

From the moment she hoisted the equipment into the trunk of the taxi, while the driver looked on through the rearview mirror, she had an inkling that just a backpack and a change of clothes would have sufficed. She already dreaded the prospect of lugging the bulky case with her. The feeling only amplified when she shuffled into the backseat. She peered back at the penetrant eyes that scanned her every movement in the mirror, framed by wiry eyebrows like antennas.

It seemed silly to take yet another 45-minute taxi ride to Cipher Falls rather than take a bus or borrow a car, but she didn't drive, and a two-and-a-half-hour circuitous route on the New Stockholm bus network was past her comfort threshold with so many intrusive thoughts as companions.

Despite the fact that she'd worn disconnected earphones, for their soothing whoosh and to signal her unavailability, the driver whose name she forgot as soon as he said it—Roshan, Ivan?–struck up a conversation.

"Nice weather we're having, finally?"

Gauntlet thrown. Very well, Roshan, Ivan? she thought. Expecting that it would soon be over, she humoured the driver whose eyes crinkled into gentle half moons.

"Yes, finally."

He grinned and revealed an endearingly imperfect mouth, teeth like a warped barn door, while he expounded on the intricacies of the nice weather they were currently having, as opposed to the weather they were previously having and the usual weather they might have.

As soon as there was a lag in the conversation, she started to angle her face toward the window, ready to diffuse her attention, maybe recline into silence. But he flashed that smile at her again and unraveled another thread of conversation.

"You are a resident of Cipher Falls?"

Five awkward seconds passed while she wondered what to tell him.

Briefly, she considered fabricating a story about hiking or birdwatching around the bay, but she couldn't imagine a version of her life in which she would be couched in that level of idleness, nor was she someone who could lie coherently on the spot, so she opted for a version of the truth.

"Erm no, I'm meeting someone about a project."

"Ah, what line of work are you in?"

"Films. I'm a filmmaker."

"What kind of filmmaker?"

His eyebrows lifted immediately, as if he was pleased to have found a point in common between them, point being that everybody likes films. She dreaded that kind of question, and its follow-ups, and how he seemed to think that he was benefitting her by probing for specifics.

"Documentary."

"Anything I'd have seen?"

"Possibly not."

"What are you working on at the moment?"

"Have you heard of the DCI urban renewal project?"

"Ah yes, that whole thing? I heard they're turning it into green space. Or was it condos? Yeah, I heard something on the radio. Sounds like it will be good for the economy, and the locals too. They are lucky for this. Anyway, those terrorists will do anything to devalue a good thing...."

Another denialist. Zeynab could usually spot them from a mile away by their look of contented normalcy and aggressive cheer, but she'd been sucked in by this one's agreeable manner. She noticed that while talking, he maintained his smile, but that his tone had shifted to a more forceful pitch.

Sometime in between the downtown core and the garment district, a series of crumbling warehouses and perpetually vacant storefronts, he recounted to her in convoluted detail how his people hadn't started off as white but had petitioned to become white, and how, despite initially hard times, he'd managed to start a business and put his three—now—adult children through school, one an engineer, another a dental hygienist, and also, an esthetician. Enumerated in order of prestige, all of them now sufficiently white and middle class–demonstrating the intractable nature of assimilation, its potential for triumph over... what, exactly?

Dear god, this man is whitesplaining assimilation to me, she thought to herself as she smiled politely, one earphone in, the other dangling over her shoulder.

It takes a certain kind of grit to ignore someone in close quarters. How can one, in good conscience, turn away from a fellow human being, especially when common courtesy suggests that one should build some sort of rapport over the business of driving and being driven somewhere, exchanging pleasantries and finding commonalities? But before he could add another word, she turned away from the man and inserted her other earbud for the thirtysome minutes that remained of the ride. Despite the fact that he bristled at this, and that his driving from that point was dashed with rage, Zeynab took the hard stops and swervy corners in stride, dissociated, and only removed the earphones again once they reached her destination.

She paid hastily without making additional eye contact.

"Take care," he said. "Be safe."

"No worries," she said, scrambling out of the car as fast as possible.

*

A staycation in Cipher Falls, on the other side of New Stockholm. High rises. Haphazard construction sites. Hostile architecture. What felt like the bottom or margin of the city was actually its core, a rocky patch of land that crumbled around a body of water. The yolky center. No falls to speak of, but always a sensation of tumbling, perhaps from an energetic imprint left 300 years ago when an ambush led to the comeuppance of a minor colonial garrison, repayment for the massacres of Indigenous communities. The military theatre was situated at the mouth of the bay, where the troops didn't see the retaliation coming and spilled off the cliff to their death, seven kilometres from the lock through which Zeynab was jamming a key.

As soon as she stepped into her short-term rental, an old paranoid habit told her to stop and search it. Behind the bed frame. At the far edge of the ceiling. Under the coffee table. Under the armchair cushions. Every inch of the balcony. Behind the generic landscape painting.

When she'd had enough, she sat on the balcony and kicked off her shoes, wiggled her toes, took a few minutes to register the stink of her feet and remembered that she'd forgotten the goddam gear case in the taxi trunk.

She raged about it in the shower. Standing under a trickle of achingly low water pressure, she strained to listen to sounds in the next room. Throughout, she kept an eye on the butter knife she had placed on the soap dish.

Toweling off with her back to the wall, she bucked and scrambled to cover herself as soon as she was in the direct line of sight of a neighbour in the building across the street. He leaned on his bannister and sipped his coffee. When she crept back to the window to assess the extent of the view, he returned the eye contact, positively glared in a way that suggested that he was not only offended but annoyed, and more so than her, by her exposure.

*

Someone, a bubbly acquaintance, had explained to her that the only real way to understand a place is to get lost in it. At the time, the comment had struck her as the vacuous kind of shit people post on social media. But now, faced with the same task, she endured the same exercise, stumbling, groping, stopping every few minutes as she walked toward the bay along an absence of footpath, cross-checking the street signage with her phone map, losing her bearings just as soon as she found them. Without her usual reference points, she felt she was like a creature circling a concrete maze, possibly at the mercy of giants who watched from above.

Resenting her disorientation, she refused to use her smartphone or ask for directions. Not even at the bus shelter, where she stood bashfully in front of the map, trying to decipher her route, blocking the entrance as passengers and buses came and went. Her reptilian brain engulfed her in a tingle of panic and hypervigilance, to the extent that she leaned against the pole for support. From that vantage point, she watched other people board and disembark, and could only see, mirrored in their faces, her own alienation, to which she responded with a feedback loop of increasing awkwardness.

But eventually, she made it to a hair braiding appointment at the hairstylist's apartment. Six hours of sitting between a stranger's thighs, an intimate commitment that lasted much longer than anticipated and left her with a fierce headache and a taut scalp that stretched her eyes out like a cat's. And damn, did she look good.

To quell the headache, she ducked into a decrepit movie theatre, where she purchased a ticket to a romantic comedy, featuring a stressed-out white girl who quits her job to find herself in another country. She sat at the very top section, near the aisle, close to the entrance. Feet slung on the back of the seat ahead of her, she let the sequence of images wash over her. The melodrama portrayed on screen illuminated and played on the angles of her face and replenished her energy. Eventually, she relaxed into the film, always with an eye to the exit.

She spent the first night of her stay with the apartment lights on, sprawled in bed in her underwear, letting her one change of clothes air out while scribbling in a notebook. For supper, she consumed beer from the corner store and ate a sleeve of saltines, the tops of which she scraped to cut the salt content. Her notes contained little about the project itself, but rather ephemera like phone numbers, dates, place names, doodles in every margin, and blackened spaces inside the Os and As.

She peered out the balcony window, partly hoping to see the neighbour again, if only to catch sight of a familiar presence, but his curtains were drawn. With the tip of her tongue, she located a kernel of popcorn between her molars.

The next morning, the neighbour was back at it, sipping coffee on the balcony, this time with someone she assumed to be an overnight visitor. Zeynab was there to receive them, having installed herself at the flimsy plastic table and chair on her balcony. She averted her gaze from them and munched on the last of the crackers and drank lukewarm unsweetened tea, the acid of which provoked momentary nausea. This time, while the guest nuzzled against the neighbour's neck, Zeynab looked at him with a cold open stare.

*

She had plans to meet a subject at a fast food place situated 20-minutes inland from the bay. It was mighty bustling. She stood at the entrance, making awkward eye contact with the clientele as they pushed past the entrance.

As Zeynab waited, she mumbled her standard introduction to herself, which was a repetition of the copy-pasted emails she sent. *Thanks for making time to meet. I've reached out to others who are affected by the so-called "urban renewal" project, people like you, many of whom you may know personally.* Cautiously, as one would avoid looking directly into the sun, she would leave out any words that evoked violence or pain, anything that would spook a potential informant. The closer they were to harm, the more she affected neutrality. She'd done otherwise and paid for that rookie mistake in an earlier project. That potential interviewee seemed so alienated, he'd stopped answering her texts.

Today's interviewee appeared across the street on a mountain bike, wearing a hat and sunglasses, presumably to protect his identity. She recognized the locs that reached down to his bum from a grainy Internet photo she'd studied. Doudou Laguerre. Zeynab greeted him with a wave. He hesitated a moment, chained his bike to a telephone pole, walked over and grabbed for the door, all while barely acknowledging her.

At the counter, she paid for his number three combo and her coffee.

She followed him to a table that, you could already tell by sight, had an oily surface. He ate and she sipped in silence. Within minutes, she found herself balking at his presence. It took a few deep breaths to pinpoint the source of her hesitation while he scarfed his fries. Beyond his standoffishness, it was the potency of their relationship, of which he seemed unaware. How much they needed each other. His political mission. Her institutional access. Yet he seemed unaware of himself as an outsider or underdog. That pain, evident in the comely eyes that looked at her across the table, was a means through which he made sense to himself. And yet, it was also a powerful vehicle for social change. And that was something that belonged to his community, to the collective, to history, and in some small way to her.

"What led you to me?" he asked suddenly, reaching for his drink.

Zeynab delivered the same speech she gave everybody, all while scowling to herself, lost in her own script, plunging into an amenable paradigm of events that she had worked and reworked in the last weeks. A viaduct. A dog park. An expressway. How do you reckon with the impending construction of an infrastructural feature that will trace a convenient little shortcut for the rest of the population, and in the process, strike through the heart of your community? All this, in the name of public interest, the greater good, a construct in which some don't exist, in that they are the lesser evil? As she spoke, she found herself adjusting her tone to match his mood. Cool and direct.

His hands bore the evidence of a vigorous physical life, something about which she knew little. Scarred, gnarly, and not unattractive. They were ornamented with heavy iron rings on each knuckle, even the left index finger that was missing a tip. She leveled her gaze at his face to hide her ogling.

In the booth behind them, a guy with a default outside voice described the finer points of a mushroom trip to a companion who did not seem to care. She relaxed during pauses in his chatter and flinched whenever he started up again. When she resurfaced, he stared back at her and let an excruciating silence grow between them, one she immediately tried to fill.

"Of course, you don't have to say anything on camera... yet. It's just a few conversations to get to know each other and...."

"How do you mean?"

"I mean, like, unstructured interviews or we could just meet up again or talk on the phone."

"I don't do media." He said this in a way that was kind but challenged her, as if he was trying to provoke a reaction.

Right at that moment, she thought to lash out, dismiss his protectiveness as paranoia. Unconsciously, she mistrusted people who chose to forego institutional or collective affiliation. It seemed suspect to her, the mark of someone who had so little to lose that they didn't care what others thought of them. But she controlled the urge. She might need him.

"Let's get out of here," he declared after he finished his last fry, rising from his seat. He walked out the door without waiting to see if she'd follow him.

As they walked, Zeynab noted to herself that he conveniently held his bike between them, like a shield. In spite of this distance, she kept the step and hung onto his every word, craving more. Momentarily, she even forgot to keep track of the direction in which they were headed. Except that it was a path circling the bay, guarded by a shelf of steep spiky rock that almost protected the beach from view. If that's what you could call that narrow patch of pebbles.

Only then did she find her bearings. It was as if the challenging hike demanded it. Mindfulness, deep breathing, and watching one's step. She slipped into a steady pace and followed him to a point up the bay. A breathtaking midday view of the city, foregrounded by Cipher Falls. He squinted toward a point.

"That's my place over there."

"Oh?"

*

I'm going to fuck this up, she thought as they tumbled into his bed, 40-minutes later.

But now, all of a sudden, she grasped him more fully than she could have otherwise. It was in the way he adjusted his posture, swayed into her, leaned in and out to generate propitious angles, submitted himself to her searching hands, agreed on a rhythm that guided them both into a surge of mutual understanding.

By this time, her body odour had bloomed to a full stench, which he didn't seem to notice. His body smelled of earth, and his locs, some sort of vapourous oil, like tea tree or eucalyptus. Also, the whiff of stale cannabis from the restaurant, she realized, came from him. His indifference evaporated until there was just light refracted in his eyes, relief, and the drip of a loose tap somewhere in his apartment.

She spent the rest of the afternoon lounging at his place, a veritable excavation site.

It was also his workspace, as she could see from his drawing table and graphics tablet. He owned multiple sets of cookware, dog-eared magazines, a broken bicycle, a record player, a wall-to-wall record collection, and a trove of filled sketchbooks.

Their breadth and intensity surprised her. She had expected his artistic practice to be casual, at best, or a folksy manifestation of his activism, and reproached herself for her snap judgment. He had a substantial oeuvre that might only be discovered after his death or junked by an indifferent landlord.

The subjects varied from mythical beings to abstract motifs. Among the illustrations, one stopped her. A portrait of a siren. More sketch than photorealist. Craggy charcoal lines. Quite sensible despite the jumbo comic book boobs. Something about their intensity conveyed fury, or the feeling of a hastily scrawled shopping list. Incidental beauty. She reflexively drafted notes around it in her mind.

While Zeynab continued to flip through the drawings, Doudou placed a steadying hand on her shoulder, a detail that somehow made it into her notes later. Even mentally, she couldn't help but chronicle his every movement.

She was intrigued about something in his manner, a protectiveness around his illustrations. As she turned the pages, he seemed to gauge her expression, taking it in as a conclusive assessment. In response, she guarded her own reaction, tempered it to deflect that responsibility.

When she handed the sketchbook back to him, he cradled its spine as one would a baby's head. She wanted to laugh at how off-kilter he looked in white socks and briefs carrying the oversized book.

"You know, I had doubts about meeting you," he said, interrupting her thoughts.

"Yeah?"

Without breaking eye contact, he sat down on a trunk that doubled as a chair and retrieved a joint from behind his ear. She briefly wondered if it had been there the whole time, then approached him and knelt between his legs, elbows propped on his knees. He lit the joint and addressed her through a cloud of smoke.

"Yeah sis. I had my doubts. I used to think it would take some advocacy to change our situation, that the moment enough folks knew about the plight of my people, there would be a reckoning. I looked you up before we met. I've seen your stuff—the recordings and all that. I wanted to meet up with you and call you out to your face, expecting another rapacious journalist. My friends told me, 'Doudou, don't bother.' But the way you showed up without a camera… I mean, I wouldn't go as far as to say that it won me over, but it made me want to talk to you, at least, see how it went. But then, I saw how timid you looked, a bit wet around the ears, not to mention being a womb-an."

"A–what?"

"But you know what the problem is? You all want transparency. And you. Worst of all. You, with your unblemished brown skin and your bleeding heart. You do the job for them. By wanting to make everything limpid, clarified, crystal clear... for what? For whom? What do you and allathem plan to do with all that knowing? You'll be sitting there in your little corner, knowing everything while everybody eats shite. Like you doing us a favour. You think I like to consume that junk at the Dunbar? Combo number four?"

"Three," she offered meekly.

"Three, four, five, I don't give a fuck. Guess where we can find the nearest yam, plantain, or bag of rice? That's right. Nowhere near close enough. Anyway, the best way to eat good here is to eat at home."

He was, quite literally, talking down to her. But she remained careful not to stare too openly. She'd been told before, by friends, that despite her wide-eyed look, her gaze had something predatory to it, perhaps in the darting back and forth of her irises. On this tightrope, she feared that emoting too much or too little would disrupt the flow of his confession. To counter it, she relaxed her face, letting the weed smoke ripple over her.

"Ultimately, if we're going down, so are they. What's a little explosion, or a bit of sugar poured down the fuel tank of a bulldozer, an excavator, a backhoe, against the lives of thousands of children, mothers–queens, kings... and gender dissenting royalty?

"They built this system on the empty spiritual foundation of earth, its extraction. A hole that constantly needs to be filled, always generating other holes, tearing at the fabric of organic life. Perceiving things, only with the aim to destroy them. Creating an 'up' so there can be a 'down.' Fabricating a heaven so that they can send people to hell.

"What they don't know is that we're free, regardless of what they think, do, or say. We're free. We been free. Our spirits will continue to be so, whether they're encased in flesh or floating through the motherfucking ether.

"This earth they're after? We're constantly leaving monuments to our greatness on it. I mean, DCI, man, I can't even— do you know what this highway-building contract earns them? It's an immaterial figure when you compare it to the spiritual and sociocultural legacy of my community."

There was a pause. He reached down, cupped her chin. With those mangled hands. Not wanting to interrupt the flow of his confession, she bit her lip and resisted the urge to ask clarifying questions.

"My one consolation. Even if it doesn't work out and we all get ousted. Really. Truly. Is that even if the world thrives on thinking of us as small, insignificant, there's a real bigness to our smallness. We're really no different from the stars. Do you know how big a star is? Some of them are bigger than Cipher Falls, if not the entire city. Some of them could swallow up most of our solar system. And yet, if you look at molecules, viruses, undersea microbes.

They're as direct a reflection of the stars as you can get on this Earth. See, our ancestors knew this.

"But too many of you are thinking on a caucasian humanoid scale. Small and linear. Flat as their asses. All the while, this planet of ours—she is immense and voluptuous. Those who claim to be the biggest and most important elements in our society have completely misjudged their relevance to the universe. Forgetting where they exist in the equation. Missing out. Too damn busy making things transparent.

"Anyway. Here we are now."

He said this with a pointed look. It was unclear whether his declaration was of an erotic or professional nature, but at this point, it felt to her as if it drew from the same wellspring.

He looked down at his fingers. Already, his joint had burned down to a roach. And suddenly, it occurred to her that she had overstayed her welcome. She got up and gathered her scant things while he gave her instructions on how to take the bus back, articulating those instructions so slowly to her that it felt offensive.

Standing at his doorway, she had the urge to confiscate something of his, a pencil, an umbrella, any material proof of their interaction. But she would be back. Just before walking out the door, she turned around, offered a limp hug, which she immediately regretted.

In the stairway, it finally occurred to her to check her phone. A missed call and a voicemail. A 1-800 number. Temple pressed against the window, she listened to the nasal message on the bus ride back. They'd found her gear case, which she could retrieve at the taxi company headquarters during office hours, which would end in an hour and a half.

A few stops away from her sublet, a pang of hunger made her regret not having eaten one of the combos at the restaurant, or at least taken one to go. A quick check on her phone revealed that all nearby grocery stores were closed. She'd lost track of the time. In a sweep of a dusty corner store's aisles, she opted for a couple of beers, a can of tuna, and another box of cream crackers on which to spread it.

As soon as Zeynab reached her apartment, she cracked open a can of beer and pocketed a handful of crackers to consume on the bus, right after splashing water on her face, armpits, and crotch. She would shower after she returned from the taxi headquarters.

That evening, she took another taxi, with a different driver who took her on an alternate route toward the city centre, foregoing the scenic view for a stretch of highway that looked like another city, any city. When she checked her phone, there was a single text from Doudou.

"Come again soon x."

Point & Shoot

In which Maya witnesses something shocking

IMAGINE GETTING PISS on your favourite photograph. The gush of panic as you shake beads of droplets off rucked-up edges. I should've paid attention to Chekhov's whining, but I ignored him and rolled myself a cigarette instead. As always, my bones feel broken after a gig.

He made me pay for it by urinating on one of my photo albums. Had I not been there to rescue it, the fucker would have soaked through a rare image of my parents on their wedding day. In it, my mother wears a taffeta gown with beaded details down the front. Her face looks washed out behind her veil, clouded by a blotch of overexposure. My philandering-ass father wears a borrowed tux and rests a possessive hand on her shoulder. Tonton Roland, her brother, snapped the picture on a disposable camera a few moments after the ceremony. Apparently, following their civil union, he treated them to a bottle of good rum. This image holds all the clues to my mother's problems, and by extension mine.

Luckily the pigments remain intact, I discover as I dab it. Oxidized and dog-eared from thirty-odd years spent at the bottom of my mother's sewing drawer, I've rescued and preserved it in the same acid-free, lignin-free, pH-neutral box where I store all of my most valuable prints.

Otherwise, I hate wedding ceremonies. Shooting them, especially. Too stagy, too vain, too much competition with guests who get in the way of shots with their camera phones. Everybody just trying to grab a piece of the newly indebted couple as they feign smiles through tight faces. Someday, a future civilization will mistake wedding pictures for documentation of sacrificial rites.

But I can't begrudge my only paycheque. Where would I be without Ioannis, who hooks me up with gigs? Right out of our photography programme, he's the only one who gravitated to it, just a gangly kid with a speedlight and an umbrella, asking dysfunctional clans to cheese in the midst of big fat Greek weddings. We mocked him back then, but he's the only one among us who's solvent, except for those who sold out to work in HR or whatever.

I knew I should have turned down his last-minute request yesterday when he called me into a garish reception at the port. They'd decorated a shipping container in a mint and gold color scheme that defiled my retina. The physical strain and distractions were such that I tripped over the cranky four-year-old ring bearer and slammed into a waiter who spilled a tray of salads with such a clatter that the mother of the bride looked ready to uppercut me to a parallel dimension.

Minutes later, Ioannis waved me over to the parking lot. I followed him, expecting him to chew my ass out, but instead he offered me a cigarette and spoke to me cordially, like it was teatime and not T-minus ten minutes from the cake cutting.

"Hey man, listen... sorry about that! I don't know what my—"

"How's the studio practice? Still on that art shit?" He blew a cloud of smoke from the corner of his mouth.

I shrugged.

"I'm meeting someone about a potential job tomorrow."

"A gig?"

"Yeah, some Zeynab Abdi."

"Oh snaps. Zeynab?"

"You know her?"

"Good luck with that."

"What? What do you know about her?"

"Look her up."

"Of course."

"And listen, from this point forward, why don't you just tap out? The only thing left on the shot list is wedding cake and the dollar dance. I've got it."

"Hey buddy... You know I need the work."

Ioannis flicked his cigarette butt into a planter and rubbed the stubble on his chin. When did he get like this? The fidgety kid I knew in photography class has become an overseer.

"I guess you can retouch the set this time. Keep it standard. No quirky stuff."

"Deal."

Late that night, when I get back to my apartment, I find Chekhov sitting on my laptop. Warmed it right up for me.

This is my favorite part, processing the images. I only retouch at night. The stillness and muted sounds all lead to clearer images. Fewer disruptions mean that I can home in on a gesture, pick up on the undertones of flesh, perceive everything with x-ray vision. That's why I painted my bedroom white. I usually fall asleep while staring at my bare walls, where my eyes project the negatives of images and allow me to enjoy the views while dozing off in the early hours of the morning. I rarely dream anyway.

*

Late into the next day, I wake up groggy, tidy up my place, and fill up on the dinner rolls and butter that the caterers let me take home. Another perk of these gigs. The rolls soften a bit if you microwave them for a few seconds with a pat of butter. I can already tell I'll need the energy.

It takes me three buses and a metro ride to get to our meeting point, one of those cafés with inane shit like vintage license plates displayed on the walls. They're playing an ingratiating acoustic remix of Nancy Wilson's "How Glad I Am," a damned mockery. I comment as much to Zeynab when I settle at the table across from her.

"You're very acute, aren't you?"

"You mean astute?"

"There it is."

Within the first five minutes of meeting her, I'm perturbed by her vibes. I mean, that glazed look in her eyes. She drinks her coffee black and rambles in whispery tones about gentrification this, oral history that.

I looked up her stuff online before we met. This bitch needs therapy. One of her documentaries, I swear to god, consists of a screaky field recording that goes on for three hours straight. I only lasted for the first half hour before tapping out. Little else but screeching and grunting. It's not that I don't get or like artists who make mausoleums out of their trauma. What grates me is when they also choose to make their work inaccessible. Don't even get me started on the synopsis, which is unintelligible. Complete gibberish. How is it that these types get all the grants?

I intend to find out. She'll probably want me to shoot analogue, which makes sense for still photography, but would be a pain for a doc shoot. A total luddite. I'm no hype beast, but I can tell from her outfit that she probably wears homemade tampons.

It was a complete mistake to order the carrot cake. It looks more like a veggie casserole than dessert. And what's with all the flecks of carrot leaves? What is this café? I take a bit out of the corner and spit it right out. Cardboard vegan shit.

"So what kind of interviews do you intend to shoot?"

"It's complicated. I don't have any lined up yet. Also, I'm not looking to do conventional interviews. At least not for the first little while. My hope is to build a rapport, just bear witness, and then eventually we might start to bring equipment around."

"No interviews? So you don't need me yet?"

"Of course I do. I'd like to keep exploring the city, maybe get some B-roll. Mainly exteriors. But ultimately, what I'm looking for is presence."

I resist rolling my eyes, if only to secure the gig.

"What kind of medium do you work in? Digital? Analogue?"

"Both. I like the ease of digital, but I usually prefer the feel of film for the physical memory."

Aha.

"Speaking of which, do you have your own equipment?"

"What's your budget? I can make a few calls, but it depends."

Truth be told, I'd have to make more than a few calls about a camera. It's a damned shame I've burned all my bridges in New Stockholm. I swear, you've gotta have your own equipment-depot guy. Most of them have skid marks in their baggy boxer-briefs, but just because they're given the keys to the backroom of some institution, they reign over everybody like feudal lords.

"What's your timeline, exactly? I have a few shoots lined up throughout the rest of the month, but I'll—"

"Can you travel with me on Friday?"

"Friday?"

"Friday."

So she just wants someone to follow her around Cipher Falls for however long. I think about the wedding Ioannis had booked for us Friday. How sweltering it will be.

Forecast says 35° C. The only thing worse than a rained-on wedding is a sunny one. That's when wedding parties are at the height of their nerves. I've seen a bride lose her shit and break her husband's dick because he wouldn't pose with his in-laws. She just reached out and twisted until it snapped like a breadstick.

"Look, your project sounds interesting, but—"

"It's paid, of course."

"Yeah, sure, I understand th—"

"A thousand a day."

"Can you put that in writing?"

*

When I get back to my apartment, I notice that Chekhov still hasn't budged from his spot by the window. Not much of a view, other than the empty lot with a FOR RENT sign across the street. I walk over to pet him and check his breathing. Old bastard is hanging by a thread.

He freaks out. This is bananas, I tell myself, as I pull fur out of my mouth. Simply bananas. There's no way I can work with Zeynab, I tell myself, but at least it's better than trailing another bridezilla.

*

We meet early on Friday morning to pick up the car she borrowed, a Subaru Baja. Impractical jalopy, like a cross between a truck and a sedan, but it rolls well, and immediately begins to grow on me.

She lives in a high-rise building in the part of town where you're only ever a few minutes' stroll from a place where you can buy an outfit for your dog. That's what people do here. They stroll.

For some reason, as we crawl through traffic, I feel jittery around her. I attempt to make conversation, but she barely responds, just stares straight ahead, so I relax into the stillness.

We push through for another 40 minutes until we finally hit the highway. My eyes settle on a distant point that fills up with various things—an electric blue Honda, a silver Chevy, a crushed rodent.

I rarely make it to this side of town. And why should I? I have no relations here anymore except for a third cousin who never made it out the hood. A quaint place, sure. But you don't just hang out in a neighbourhood like this. Not if you don't have people here. And there's that nauseating septic odor that hits us a quarter of the way there. We have to roll the windows shut, even though the AC's broken. The sky, which started off clear and sunny, is shrouded with clouds that swirl in a way that feels foreboding.

At my request, we stop at a corner store for a case of Gatorade and come across a small congregation of elders by the door who smoke and stare at us, like we're on TV.

She stares back at them.

"You ready to jet?"

"Give me a sec."

Before I can intervene, she walks over to one of them, exchanges a few words, and to my surprise, he follows her back to the car and slips into the backseat.

"We've booked our first interview," she says, as she buckles her seatbelt.

"What? I thought we were—"

"Change of plans," she says, shrugging. "Just follow his directions."

As we drive off, I peer at the guy in the rear-view mirror and back at her. This bitch lacks protocol. Will it always be like this?

He directs us down a main artery that's blocked by so many construction signs, you almost have to spiral in on yourself to get somewhere. We finally reach a more residential stretch of road, at which point he asks me to brake in front of a dingy building, a church.

The church sits right in front of a picturesque grove, the kind of shit that would frame a talking head shot beautifully, but instead, she lets the guy unlock the door to the building.

"He's a deacon here," she mouths.

The vibes are dense. If I had to scout a location for a snuff film, this would be it.

She has me set up the camera in an obscure corner. I install a backdrop and do my best to direct the light by bouncing a few rays that infiltrate from a fortunately placed skylight, but I already fear that these visuals are going to be murky as fuck.

As they clear the area, I start to unpack the equipment. Ioannis, bless him, let me borrow his camera and lighting kit, but not without ragging on me for bailing.

"Don't let me lose you, kid," he said.

Kid? I'm pretty sure I'm five years his senior.

I notice a rip in the background. Groaning, I rummage through my backpack until I find a roll of duct tape and patch it up. It's practically unnoticeable, but you can still see it on the monitor, in the lower right-hand corner of the frame.

And then I wonder about the light.

Whoever owns or haunts this place could stand to wipe down the surfaces every now and then. Even so, the amount of dust suspended in the air diffuses the light like no other. The sunlight that streams through the window shifts ever so slightly and, suddenly, the room is diaphanous, like fog machine-quality, without the pain of rental, fluid, and insurance fees.

I reach into the equipment bag and retrieve a 50 mm lens and a collapsible softbox. With a few adjustments, this setup could provide a soft overlay of light that would mimic the misty veil of memory.

When they return, I invite the guy to sit on his mark, a bench. He does so uneasily.

"Would you like a Gatorade?" I offer, as if it's chamomile tea.

"Nah."

Already he seems afraid to open up. That much is clear by the forceful way he looks back at the camera, head on, like he's ready to initiate a fistfight with the lens.

Interesting reflex. Most people conflate on-camera interviews with intimacy. They like the attention paid to them and get attached so quickly. I cringe, thinking about those first awkward moments after a shoot, when I'm accounting for the things I wish I could unhear. How flustered people get from a listening ear, how eager they remain for it after they've gotten a taste.

Zeynab positions herself to the right of the camera, inviting his gaze toward her, although his eyes flit back to me occasionally.

"Can you tell me a bit about yourself?"

"What kind of things do you mean?"

"Like where did you grow up?"

"Not too far from here. A couple of kilometres away. It was livelier then, I guess. More youngsters. After we were done with chores, we would hang around up the road..."

"Do you live with your family?"

"It's just me now. The rest of them moved to other parts of the city, but they..."

The rest of his words fly past me. He talks with his hands, some of the roughest I've ever seen, and never lets up, except to break eye contact with Zeynab and look right into the camera, at me. Kind of a nightmare to keep his eyes in focus. Quite the face. Complicated shapes like a geological formation. Cleft chin. High cheekbones, a forehead that juts out and reflects the overhead light.

We get five minutes into it before I realize that she doesn't know how to interview for shit. The guy is incredibly tense, just clammed up inside his own head, hasn't uttered a coherent sentence, and she just keeps talking over him, yammering on in long paragraphs like it's her thesis defense. I've never seen anything like it.

But then, amidst the stumbling around, the unexpected happens. The guy starts to huff and puff, until he's fully hyperventilating, and then he just breaks down into tears, and there he is, just about melted in his seat. Face just running with snot. He just collapses into himself, like an island ravaged by a hurricane of human emotion.

Now I'm ready to cut the camera and am waiting for her to comfort him, or at least, address his discombobulation, but she's not even looking at him. After a couple of uncomfortable minutes, she signals at me to cut the camera, with an almost flippant gesture.

*

After we drop the guy off where we found him, I turn to her.

"What the hell was that?"

She shrugs, like a maniac, and looks at me with those enormous eyes. A beautiful monster. Her methods creep me out. And to what end? Is she going for pure grit? Misery porn? I may be broke, but I don't want to be part of some gonzo project.

We spend the rest of the day creeping around the neighborhood. Until I get hungry. At which point we stop by a fast food joint where I pick up a combo number five burger meal with two extra patties. We sit in the Subaru in a vacant parking lot while I struggle to keep the meats in the buns. When that fails, I pick out the ingredients and eat them individually.

Then we both turn to people-watching. Not much to it. People working. People walking. People walking to work. No dillydallying here. At least, not with all those cop cars patrolling. It's a locus of industry and going places. It manifests in their faces. Nobody makes eye contact, which you would expect the opposite of in a tight-knit neighbourhood, but no. All scowls. When he catches me staring, one guy even shakes his head, a nonverbal question I can't answer. Bold-facedly, Zeynab eyeballs everybody, as if she could decipher something accurate about them just by looking.

*

Our final stop, at Zeynab's request, is the toilet of a bay that looks away from the city, as if in shame. As soon as we step out of the car, she lights a joint and asks me to bring along my camera.
"What's next? Do you need B-roll?"

"What do you mean, 'what's next?'"

"For the story you're pursuing. Can you walk me through what's happening here?"

She ignores my question and passes me the joint, which I decline.

"It's not about what's happened, but what's happening."

"What?"

"Look around you. What do you see?"

"A shitty city beach. Say that ten times fast."

"Look again. You know, if you just listened, you'd probably figure it out."

"Figure out what?"

"Weren't you listening?"

"Listening to what?"

"We're just here to bear witness."

"Sure, whatever... Hey, shouldn't we head back? It's going to get dark soon. Plus, my gear isn't insured."

"Could you shut up for a minute?" A vein crops up on her forehead. First time I've seen her display such enthusiasm.

I shudder, remembering the long stretch of highway. Chekhov is probably waiting for me, getting more anxious by the second. I convinced my sister to stop by and check in on him, but I wouldn't put it past him to take a rage shit on my shoes.

The sun hangs low over the bay while I set up a few wide shots. We've been standing there for a good half hour, and I'm getting colder and hangrier by the second. Positively drained. I could reach out and strangle her. She's lucky she hasn't paid me already.

It's still light out, but the moon starts to peak in the opposite corner of the bay, like a watermark. I'm about to turn back when I notice a glint beneath me. The beach is covered in jagged stones and shattered shells that you can't help but step on for a satisfying crunch.

The only sounds are the waves of the bay, the wind picking up, and my labored breathing. She bends down and picks up a handful of stones. She rattles them in her hands and looks at them so closely that her eyeball practically grazes the little mound.

I bend over and grab a handful myself. Much softer than you would expect, like marbles or pearls. On an impulse, I throw it at her, and then brace myself for the worst, but she immediately giggles, like a kid. She throws me back a handful, but misses. I return the favour with a quick pitch that hits her in the face. She resolutely grabs for another pile and gets me right in the chest, so that we're both covered in it now. I drag my fingers across the soil and rake an even bigger mound to fling at her, when my finger catches on something gooey. Against my better judgment, I reach for it and squint in the last light and catch sight of heterogeneous textures, like a bunch of eyes that make me feel trypophobic. I bring it to my ear, as if expecting the woosh of the ocean or some other screaming kind of white noise that would raise every hair on the back of my neck. For what feels like a good hour, we pad around the beach in a daze, looking at our feet, lifting shit, putting it down.

I smell it before I see it—a biting scent like gloom wafting from the left side of the beach. After I check under the soles of my shoes, I turn to Zeynab to assess whether or not she smells it too. Her head is in the clouds. She marches while looking out at the bay, toward the other side of the beach. As we continue to walk ahead, toward the rock wall, the smell becomes more definitive, like the opening chorus of a song.

And just as I approach a patch of trees growing out of the bluffs, I catch sight of an irregularity in the pattern of evergreens that hang there, a supine mass hanging from a cluster of branches, as if it was left out to dry. As I squint harder, trying to process what I'm seeing, I gradually realize that, why yes, that is usually how a torso connects to hips, and indeed, that would be a hand connected to an arm, to a shoulder, to a chest, and that is indeed a human body hanging facedown in the branches, splayed out, like some sort of fallen superman.

We stand there frozen, for I don't know how long, processing the discovery in front of us until, finally, it sinks in that we are as complicit as the sand, the stones, the shells, and all the landscape around us in these circumstances. Powerless to alter it, we can only gaze.

It doesn't occur to me that the sun is setting, that this corpse is decaying, that we should call someone, because I'm useless at practical things, yet well-equipped to look, to analyze, to take in this scene and consume its beauty, a complicated allure undermined by its stink, a wet stench that makes my skin crawl. There are some things you would like to unsee but can't, and there are times you want to rewind back to a former innocent state of trucking down the highway, arguing over a playlist, hurtling toward a nightmare. I get why fragile characters faint in outdated movies. All I want is for vertigo to overtake me, buckle my knees, collapse me into my own softness or a pair of supportive arms, rather than to ask myself to mobilise my last brain cells of the day and make a purposeful phone call, some sort of cry for help or useful statement, any kind of statement other than, gee, I guess the corpse had an ineffable beauty, and while my brain is going in these various directions, I realize that Zeynab is next to me, has taken my camera and documented this moment.

sad hot bitches make love to shower heads (but draw the line at rainfall models)

In which Phyllida sabotages a job hunt

Time Management

THE TROUBLE WITH mornings is that they're not long enough. By the time your spirit seeps out of the dreamworld. By the time your toes curl in and out of attention. By the time the birds outside your window chirp their call and response: Phylliiiida? Phyllidaaaa! By the time you pull back the curtains on a new day. By the time your breakfast onions start to caramelize. By the time.

Logistics

Do I miss The Dunbar? Hell to the no. But I don't have the guts to go back and pick up my last paycheque. When I called, they said they'd mail it, but that I'd have to sign a form that confirmed that I received it. I think it's a trap.

Usually, I would have asked Dom to get it for me, but they went AWOL. It took me a while to catch on, until the pile of dishes in the sink got more out of hand than usual. They were spilling out onto the floor. To the point that I ate Weetabix out of a hollowed grapefruit. How was I, with these things considered, going to pay this month's rent?

Frantz was in an eerie mood when he drove me over to his condo for the first time. Oddly formal, like this was the beginning of the rest of our lives. A vein throbbed on the side of his temple while he watched me unwrap the juicer he'd meticulously gift-wrapped.

Attention to Detail

Frantz says that I'm a goddamn mess when it comes to cleaning the bathroom. He said it's like I'm trying to leave behind pieces of myself, enough stuff to generate a homunculus. That'd be handy. A miniature me living in the cupboard above the sink. I could train her to rummage through the clutter and hand me soap or a loofah once I'm settled in the bath. A glass of wine. Switch playlists.

So much goes into my bathing ritual. The siren is in the scabby stages, so I work from the torso down. You gotta do it in the proper sequence. Unscented soap. Fresh water. Hypoallergenic lotion. Three handfuls of Epsom salt. Simple as that, but it usually takes me a while to get started. First, I have to burn a bundle of lavender above the tub, until it comes to a fragrant smolder. No negative vibes should come into contact with my bathwater. Not under my watch.

The first five days of healing a new tat are critical. Each morning, I examine every inch of the area for changes, signs, and clues as to its evolution. When I'm soaking, I'm careful to limit the amount of time my new tat gets submerged. Linger too long, and the lines could bleed.

The rest of my body gets the vigorous scrubbing it deserves. I do away with that fungible layer of epidermis. My exfoliation process stimulates the flow of blood in my veins. Impatient carfuls of red blood cells hurtle through traffic jams in my body, weaving around the other donut-shaped vehicles to get to my crotch, where they're urgently needed.

Analytical Thinking

Breakfast, the ultimate chore. It's a game-changer, whenever it happens. But how do you get the proportions right and measure its timing so that it does indeed coalesce with your digestion? What thickness of coffee will carry me through the morning, through the day, what tentpole of energy boosts do I need to lie on the couch and watch the tops of suburban trees through the window, in not concentration but its opposite—a blur through my eyelashes.

Frantz likes to say that more is more is more, that you need at least five heaping tablespoons of ground coffee to hit the right concentration. The pots he brews are more like sludge than anything. You've gotta massage your throat ever so gently to make it go down. As much as I appreciate his energy, I look forward to that point every morning when he leaves the condo and leaves me the hell alone. It recalibrates the vibe.

Networking

In the same way a seashell murmurs ocean sounds, you can hear the atmosphere of Cipher Falls over the phone. Like a blast of clanging metal and horns and mothers cussing under their breath. Makes me nostalgic, hearing it against the hum of suburbia, the interior of a fridge overlayed with the distant bark of a shih tzu.

Whenever Manman clears her throat, I know she's going to ask me when I'm going to start looking for a job again. A friend of a friend of a friend of hers offered to hook me up with an office job. I think to myself: I already have a job, Ma. Calming everyone down and providing a vibe. Then I shrug and make that sad hopeful voice people expect when you talk about pretending to want to work a hypothetical job that's already killing you.

Observational Skills

At first sight, the burbs seem boring, like under-seasoned potatoes, but I could get used to the mildness of its charm. The very mildest of charm. Out here, there's a frosty sheen to the pavement and lawns and even the liquid that trickles toward the sewer grates. A particular tint, as if someone is withholding a UV ray over the atmosphere. It wasn't until I was sorting turquoise beads that I noticed the vivid shade of aquamarine that the skies here are not.

Frantz, who 100 percent thinks he rescued me from Cipher, says that I spend too much time looking at the clouds, implying that it makes me a simpleton. It's just like him to require a high-falutin breakdown of what he sees. Everything has to mean something with him. It isn't enough for a fern to just be a fern. It has to make some sort of commentary or exist as a statement, or a gradient in between. There has to be an endgame with him.

Active Listening

Frantz's anxiety has this exact shape: the clacking noise of vintage kung fu films playing on his tinny laptop speakers, just pops and punches interspersed with cries of toxic masculinity. He reminds me of a particular character, the evil halfwit in Kurosawa's *Yojimbo*, who gets more and more diabolical as his frustration increases from misunderstanding the situation he's in.

The thing is, he doesn't have a handle on how to do nothing. One minute, we've rolled and smoked a joint, bopping along to some funk, sitting there ready to watch the afternoon ramble by, the next, he's launching into some conspiracy theory about this or that, how Doudou's death was anything but accidental, ordained by the management at DCI and the city, and the Illuminati, why not, how there's a climate event on the horizon, how the trees are trying to warn us, everything to avoid shutting the hell up and just being. I've realized that the trick is to fuck him calm. It doesn't have to be a big production. Just a bit of twiddling here, a little grinding there. Enough to silence that still-small voice in his head that hollers so much that swear to god I can even hear it sometimes.

Initiative

He's hinted before that we should exchange housework for rent, even though he has verbalized the opposite, that I'm welcomed to stay as long as I needed, that *su casa es mi casa*. But let's be real, people like to say the opposite of what they mean. My only true moment of respite comes when he leaves for work and I have the condo to myself. That's when business truly begins.

I saw a liar's turquoise aura wash over Frantz, when he came home one day and found me lying down in front of reality TV. I swear the two activities were disconnected, but he seemed to take it real hard that I wasn't on my hands and knees scrubbing the floors with my back arched and my moon ass shining.

Sometimes, I wish he would pin me down on my back, cut me open, and claw out my feelings from their safe hiding place inside my gut. The ouchy and the yummy alike, leaking out in satisfying spurts. And then I want him to clean up the mess and sew me back together. Then hold me. All unprompted.

Project Management

Couldn't stand that crestfallen look on his face, so I decided to take it upon myself to paint the back door of the kitchen, using a leftover can labeled Himalayan White. By his reaction, you would've thought that I'd solved world hunger when he came home and saw the job. He ordered us dinner and fucked me good, or rather it was I who did the fucking, inconspicuously pulling the mechanism from below.

Within a few days, the paint dried and left thousands of little hairlines cracks, an unrecognizable monstrosity that reflected a blinding white light into the rest of the kitchen, such that we were always squinting in there. "Rad," he called it, like it was an on-purpose crackle finish, and not an unfortunate lack of primer. It was a mistake to paint that door. Every time I pass it, it gives me the creeps, looks like a heavily made-up clown, and I've noticed where a dead spider got painted over and immortalized in this shrine of productivity.

Relationship Building

Now, I just try to make sure I'm out when he comes home. There's not much to look at in this neighbourhood, but it's the kind of space I need from him, as much as I love him.

How we met was either kismet or a curse. I was resisting the urge to go to the government store. And then a friend suggested this reliable dealer who had a particular system, complete with aliases, a complex handshake, and a secret code. That is, if he trusts you enough to give you his address. He used to insist on meeting first-timers in crowded places, like dance parties or opening nights of big action films. We first met at a premiere of what feels like the 25th *Fast & Furious*, and spent the whole movie sucking face.

But I can feel it in my gut and pussy, their gradual cooling, that this face that I treasure will someday disappear from view. Due to me backing the hell away from him. I so want to bring him along for the ride, but I can only be his hands and heart for so long. My ass is tired.

Gahhh. I love him. I love him. I love him. i love him. i love him. i love him. i love him. i love him. i love him.

Big-picture Thinking

The thing about Frantz is that he's a tree. He's a tree that should be content to live tucked away in a corner of the forest, stretching toward the sky indefinitely, in perfect harmony with his environment. Instead he wants to be human, to act like humans do, lace up his shoes, cinch his belt, wear a necktie, pick up a briefcase and mingle in the crowd, all human-like. But all he can and should do is be the tree that he is. I've watched him be, and it's glorious. The grain of his skin-cum-bark, the rustling of his leaves, how they shed in the condo. The simple fact of his breath leaves a nice mark that fills whichever room he's in.

But the truth is that things suffer when he insists on not being his tree self, which is most of the time. I can hear the strain and cracking of his roots as he tries to hoist himself above ground and lug himself across the house, brewing his sludgy coffee that he never finishes.

It gives me a feeling of doom to hang out with him, like I'm sitting next to a ticking time bomb, except that what's waiting is not an explosion but a disintegration, a drying up of all that was good. But I have hope. I have hope.

You wouldn't expect it with most dealers, lots of them are entrenched in the market, in cahoots with secret suppliers and even more secretive process chains, but him, all the products he sells is homegrown, right down to the corny little labels he sticks on his baggies. "Frantz Inc.," as if he's a company and not some guy who bags nuggets in his living room while watching kung fu movies.

Managing Organizational Resources

His home is a garden. More garden than home. He's got so many plants, reaching and laughing all the way up to the ceiling. He doesn't use lightbulbs, just a system of mirrors that angle the sunlight right down the hallway. You would think that it would smell dank at his place, but it's all very fresh, like walking through a prairie in June.

He keeps his most prized possession, a big cheeky monstera, right above his bed frame. It's just chilling there on a floating shelf hung on the flimsy drywall that has no business staying intact, but there it is, hanging on and looking down on us as we make love. Whenever we bang up against the wall, I fantasize about it crashing down on us, but it persists on, hanging there against all odds, day after day until it's ready to obliterate our skulls during a bout of lovemaking. I have that level of faith.

Expertise

Frantz thinks I should sell my beadwork to help make ends meet. I don't know what ends exactly need to be met, but I don't care to participate in the exercise. I don't know what he sees me selling for that matter. I don't make anything. Seems like just because my face presents a certain way and I'm doing a particular motion in a fixed position, this one assumes I'm working on something I can sell. I don't work, I bead.

Even when I'm not beading, I'm actually beading. I require time and space and secrecy. I'm a spider in the corner of your shower, squirting web fluid, fabricating beauty, even if it looks to the naked eye like I'm doing nothing, even if my pants are unbuttoned and I'm binge-watching whole seasons of *Battlestar Galactica*. My potential is there, even if dormant. Even when I'm lying out on the couch and stroking myself, losing track of the time, I'm ever doing the thing. Just let me bead, godammit.

Problem Solving

He's always lost in one scheme or another that I can't keep up with. Yesterday, it was something about renewing his car insurance. Today, it's a letter he got in the mail. He's stressed, and I can hear it in the click of his jaw. Either way, he always has a dogged face about him, like he's being chased. Always at war.

Seems like the best way around it is to just wake up before he does. Wake up and greet the morning and meet the sun and the dew and the hazy sky. Make a pact with all the elements and make sure I get mine before he wakes up and gets his.

Turns out that I'm a bit of a voyeur. When Frantz is still curled up like a shrimp in his bed, I sneak out to the balcony and perch there for hours. This is where I can get the best vantage point. I've made a pact with myself to watch the speck of light that awaits me at the edge of the parking lot, just behind the neighbour's truck. First, she peaks out at me and then disappears as soon as I fix her for too long, but then pops back up full force. I've learned to just nod hello, smoke my joint, and avoid direct eye contact. I let her sit there in the periphery of my vision.

Some days, it's as if the speck of light anticipates my approach. She watches me back. Grows and changes colors. I've learned that if I ignore her and mind my own business, she will creep closer and closer to the balcony, announce herself through the window, and lurk there until I let her in for a visit. Seems like she's falling for me. It's to the point that she'll brush up against the gate, traverse the parking lot, and then sidle all the way up to the driveway. One morning, she had even edged right up to the balcony, kissing and rubbing up on the leaves of Frantz's creeping ivy plants, waiting for me to notice her. Another time, when I walked onto the balcony, she was just there, full-blown and requesting to embrace me.

I don't know what I expected to see in her face, but it turns out that she had none. She's a beauty, nonetheless. I love her for who she is, just as she is, which is to say a silhouette, an aura, inviting my gaze, daring me to let her caress my skin.

To this day, I don't know how to qualify our relationship, but I appreciate whenever we spend time sitting, touching, enjoying a steaming cup of silence. Every now and again, I work up the courage to turn and look her right in the face, and it's always a jolt of recognition, like unexpectedly catching a view of your own ass in a mirror. A joyful revelation. My only wish is for our morning hangouts to stretch longer through the day and into the evening. But she doesn't stay the night. So, I honour our morning appointments, and wait for her to come and go.

Building Partnerships

What is a morning anyway? It's just a transitional space, a joint between night and day. A moment of anticipation where one edge bleeds into another. In any case, there we were, sitting together, waiting for the day to roll in.

And Frantz, he would be in bed, curled up as ever, doing what he did best, which was to just be his tree self, a tree with roots that he was always asked to move this way or that all day, until he came home and went back to bed, doing nothing, which is what he does best, even if he doesn't know that about himself.

But one morning, he decided to switch it up for some reason, maybe a temperature change or a different dose of edibles, but he followed me out of bed and onto the balcony, carrying two cups of his thick coffee, and caught me hanging out with her, and all of a sudden, it was the three of us. Me, Frantz, and her. Perhaps not knowing how to react, she didn't disappear or run across the parking lot, but instead lingered on in a way that I wasn't expecting given how shy she had been with me and how long it had taken her to show up all the way here in the first place.

She was unfazed by him and just became even more herself. And how does something become even more herself? Especially if it is a shadow in the first place. Maybe she had crisper edges or sharper contrasts or a thicker outline. But that's expressing it as if it were ink on paper, and you see, the thing about her is that she manifested as an even denser version of herself and I'm not talking about contour or shade here, but more of a presence or feeling, like when someone says something weird and the mood in a room changes. Yes, it became even more of the presence that I'd been sitting with when I started occupying this balcony every morning at Frantz's place.

And all Frantz could do was hand me the extra cup of sludgy coffee he'd brought me, which I didn't want or need and so I turned back. If he took note of her, he never mentioned it. What he did do was break with the whole vibe by turning on one of his Kung Fu movies at full volume, loud even for him, so that all of a sudden there were all these intrusive sounds overlayed on the moment. And so I joined him on the couch and we just sat there, letting a perfectly good morning spoil away.

But she never left. The rest of that morning, I could see her through the balcony window, angled just away from me.

Conflict Management

I think he's jealous. At the time of the incident he seemed indifferent, but throughout the rest of the day there was an unspoken tension, like he was mentally telegraphing to me how upset he was, but upset in a way that he wanted me to figure out and resolve. I just brushed it off, acted like I didn't know what the matter was, as if there wasn't a weird feeling in the room. Seems like my nonchalance affected him even more, pushed him to sink even more deeply, even though we were technically just sitting there quietly on the couch. For a moment, I thought it might have been just my imagination, until he suddenly got up and yelled, "This is bullshit!" Then he stormed off into his room and slammed the door.

But that was one time. Otherwise, I've taken to going out in the middle of the afternoon, just after lunch, when I'm sure he won't be around for hours. I'll walk across the parking lot, up toward the main street, past the vacant playground, and onward until I reach the public sculpture representation of what can only be described as a puckering butthole, and there it is. A little stretch of land that has yet to be excavated like everything else, surrounded by giant mounds of sand enclosed in concrete blocks. Ideal place for a deep cry.

Interpersonal Communication

I've never seen Tamika so demoralized. Or so out of context in the burbs. She rarely betrays how she's feeling but the day I come to visit her, I can sense her sadness. While we sit in silence looking at the horizon, I can feel that her energy is off and Bijou senses it too, crying and swatting away everything, even her favourite toy. Must be a lot of pressure holding down everyone. All three of us sit there in silence, gazing into the artificial pond.

A pond is a portal. If you're not careful, you can forget which side of it you exist on. Hard to tell what's changed since I left, but I see more and more people out here who never used to come to this neighbourhood, walking their dogs on a leash or wearing splashy jogging gear, like they're making sure people know they're out for a specific reason and not aimlessly running around, and then they'll nod at me while passing by, like they're waiting for some acknowledgment. The most aggressive of their sort will formulate the words, "Gorgeous day, isn't it?" in a way that sounds like they're wondering if they should call the police on you.

One day, I waded out to the middle of the pond, which is more like a murky bog, and just stood there in the midday sun as cars zoomed past on the adjacent road. There were no fish to greet me, but still I stood there. Frantz says there are leeches, but I don't give a shit. Let them suck on me. The water is waist deep and I feel like I'm suffocating on oxygen, drowning in the toxic air of this pathetic town.

Teamwork and Cooperation

Rumour has it that the crowdfunding for Ted's facial reconstruction is going swimmingly. I can't really show my face at the Dunbar, but then again, I don't want to go back there anyway.

Frantz and everyone else I know, it's like they want to remove my hand from where it's comfortably plunged in my crotch and put me to work. Never mind that I'm already busy doing what I do, which is to say nothing, in other words, being nothing, by which I mean, being myself, a nothing-doer, which is all I know how to do.

(Said while looking in the mirror) I'm a rocky pebble. Smooth, rocky and pebbly, busily doing my thing, making children wince as they walk over me, throwing me back into the water or collecting me as the smoothest, roundest souvenir of a good time that they'll soon forget.

I'm the water, deep, expansive. Beyond language. Doing the work, reflecting the sunlight, covering what should stay covered, giving plants that shiny eel-like quality, lapping and grabbing at ankles that brush past.

I'm a child of the underworld creature who visits my dreams. She reminds me of my legacy and submerged desires. I am the silhouette, taking itself for the solid object that projects the shadow. Repeat after me: this world is an illusion.

Blue Magic

In which Mattie's pantyhose wind up in her purse

THE NERVE OF EILEEN, dragging that scoundrel here. I don't care if you're head deacon at God's own banquet hall. Ruffian is ruffian. It took me a good ten minutes to calculate that they were doing the deed and it was obvious, by the way he readjusted his prick while giving her the eye. And Eileen. Who can blame her? She must be getting that good loving, judging by her Nigerian bridal makeup and the well-oiled swing of her hips as she sashays down the aisle to deposit an offering. She nearly bopped the entire row upside the head, squeezing past them.

I would normally not leave the house, especially not on a drizzly day like this, as if God is so fatigued by our terrestrial antics that he's fast asleep and drooling over Cipher Falls. Yet I figured I couldn't decline another invitation to the church fundraiser to circumvent our relocation owing to the implantation of that beastly highway.

Incidentally, they fit in the baptism of so and so's cousin's sister's auntie's neighbour's baby.

The baby in question, a six-month old in the same aisle, has not stopped staring at me for 10 minutes straight. It used to be that babies could barely hold their own heads up or even open their eyes. How is this one looking straight down the barrel of my soul, as if performing a divination?

I've witnessed the same lucidity from a cow that my great-aunt Shirley slaughtered in her yard. It brayed and brayed long before the ax touched the nape of its neck, as if it knew all along what was to come. Aunt Shirley swore it was the shadow of Errol, a philandering neighbour, come down from town. He had disappeared just the week that the same cow had wandered into her pasture. And trust, she discovered, when she finished butchering Errol-not-the-man-but-the-Cow, that the beast had an unlikely gold tooth nestled in its jaw. I asked Aunt Shirley if she was going to report it to the authorities and ask them to investigate its dental records like what I'd seen on crime TV shows, but she chupsed me and said for what, Colombo, watch out before you get that salopri police involved. She never tried the Errol beef, but everyone who partook affirmed that he was succulent.

Anyway, I don't know if that baby is some other spirit incarnate, but I know a look that casts aspersions when I see it.

It's hot as sin here, despite the intensifying rain. All of the fans are turned on and the windows have been shut, but you can still make out the rattling on the glass and the drab city landscape. My eyes are weary looking at it. It's as if someone forgot to turn the colours on outside on some days. There's a mural on the back wall and thick drapes that modify the acoustics out of the hymnal praise. Still, it gives the impression of a sauna. I don't know for the life of me why they would allow that even given that dehumidifiers go for $29.99 at Giant Tiger. There was at least triple the amount in the donation basket that I passed along earlier. Surely, the building fund could handle it.

The gentleman in the adjacent seat is wearing a generous whiff of Gucci Uomo, complemented by spicy notes of fried herring. It's no use trying to generate a breeze by folding my programme into a fan. It's made with the same thin flimsy paper they use to print receipts on. When you fold it into an accordion, the words jumble together in a pattern that makes more sense than the gathering at hand.

My silk stockings are bunching up where my bouboun meets my inner thigh, producing an intolerable itch. It's no use joining the bathroom queue at this point. The queue threads back to another time zone. It's a procession of folk, in their Sunday best, shifting from one foot to the other, trying not to soil their fineries. I can't possibly justify spending 45 minutes in line just to eke out a vigorous scratch. I don't think I even have to use the bathroom. It was an error to skip breakfast this morning, just to face train delays. The platform was so crowded this morning, it would have only taken a sudden movement to push someone onto the tracks, a peace offering to this angry city.

For now, I'll have to be content with a discreet patdown, using a dissimulated hand underneath the hymnbook. I thought that no one was looking, but trust that the whole row of youths on the other side of me swivelled their heads toward me and started snickering. Let them wait another 20 years and see what kind of heartaches life grants them. Oh lord, this itch. Almost worse than the pastor's bellowing. Not even 10 minutes into the sermon, and he's sweating buckets and soaked through his handkerchief.

Here is Pastor Josephs' vision of Heaven: a sort of continuous banquet at which we sit meekly every day, feasting on all sorts of delicacies, but mostly preoccupied with our tender-headed Lord and Saviour-Jesus-Christ-the-White-Man, looked on adoringly by his followers, who are presumably composed of this here congregation, but only the finest of them, those who never told a lie, never cheated, never grinded their hips into someone while swaying to Kompa. This banquet is mostly ornamental. Whoever makes it there will enjoy an eternity of peace, of fellowship, of satisfaction about a life well-lived on earth, without any friction. Staged for paradise-dwellers whose privates will be as smooth as a Ken doll.

Here's the thing about his Heaven: it's suspiciously smooth, altogether too smooth, devoid of any detail or ridge of inconvenience. It reflects a life of purity in the way of these acne cleanser commercials in which pores, holes, or any sort of texture is considered an evil to be banished, scrubbed away, whitewashed, so as to resemble a Caucasian baby's backside. Now, pray tell, what does Pastor Joseph, he with his dark knuckles and 4c coils, want with a white baby's backside? This, when Sister Francine suffers from fibroids so big she look 11 months pregnant, and the Dorsinvil little ones who were taken away by children's aid, and half the congregation can't even keep their own babies safe from the white school teachers dedicated to indoctrinating in them a hatred of themselves. What possibly could he want with undeveloped white bottoms?

What about our Earthly rewards? My mansion? I want it now. My silk robe? Forthwith. This white Jesus, what is he waiting for at this point? We've already cycled through three world wars, several epidemics as well as enslavement, both acute and normalized. I demand my Earthly rewards.

It pains my heart to see Pastor Joseph strut on stage condemning sinners to Hell. What about Joan's youngest, Doudou, who used to play with explosives at the construction site and smoke ganja in the church parking lot? Baptized three years ago on this very platform. He with the locs and the little bicycle, who fell off the bluffs and mashed up his head while doing goodness knows what? Surely, he's Hellbound. And so what then? How feeble Joan has been since his passing, just a shell of herself, waistline melting, hair coming out in sorrowfully thick tufts, leaving patches of empty crop circles on her head. Surely, she doesn't want to bother with some specious banquet. She would probably rather gorge on whatever slop they serve in Hell, if it's with her son.

If Pastor Joseph is to be believed, little Doudou is basking in the depths of Hell, gnashing his teeth joyfully, smiling with his mash-up head. Or maybe they would be reunited somewhere in between, wherever it is, some sort of Catholic purgatory, filling some forms and following the course of some bureaucratic process, waiting in the triage rooms, trying to certify for an official death certificate or ID card. I'm sure Joan would wade through the mess of paperwork required to have herself transferred from Heaven to Hell, for no official purpose other than to reunite with that rowdy son of hers, may he rest in power. I'm sure she'd prefer that over sitting at some strange white man's table, eating his dry chicken for all eternity.

Honestly, I'd rather join them there than stay bored in this raggedy church, with its pathetic location and ten metro stops and two bus transfers from my apartment. I've got to hand it to them, buying this building when they did. Could've been worse. They could've continued paying extortionate rents downtown, even if these walls are rumoured to be stuffed with asbestos.

Better yet, I'll sit this one out. Heaven can wait. But if I'm speculating, I reckon I could dabble in a bit of relief. Not white, Anglo-Saxon Heaven, but a true slackening of the Hell on Earth we've been living these days.

For now, let me listen to Pastor Joseph bang on about the perils of indulging in sensuality and self-manipulation. It woefully doesn't matter that I inserted two discreet tufts of cotton into my ears, the volume of his microphone is turned up so high that it's hissing, and I can still hear him inventory a list of sins that lead to eternal damnation, which include gambling, idling, reveling in liquor, and let's not forget, fornicating outside the confines of marriage.

See how Eileen flinches at that last one. Not her man though. Too busy sucking leftover breakfast out of his own gums. Why are these fools always so concerned with what the young girls are doing with their bouboun? Joseph and Eileen's man make a fine pair. Two predators roaming up and down the church aisles.

Praise the Lord, the freshly-dedicated baby has started to cry. Sharp wails so acute that Pastor Joseph stops and glowers at the family, as if he expects them to hide the baby in the lobby until he's done sermonizing. I'd much rather hear the baby cry than continue listening to his eschatological exhortations.

Just as I consider retiring out the back door, Cynthia intervenes and leads the junior choir in a rendition of "Centre of my Joy" and I sit my behind back down for a few bars. Little Mahalia takes the solo, and from her young mouth emanates a string of pearls so fine and so precious.

Listen to me closely. Nobody is more surprised than me when I lift myself out of the pew, leaving beneath me a layer of dew from my backside on the wood grain. As I pass Eileen, her beady eyes dart toward me as if I've done something salacious, but I pay her no mind, even though my movements are jerky and mechanical and do no justice to the fluidity I feel inside. It's as if my skin, my bones, are just a constricting outline of myself, a rough shape. This vessel of my body contains who I am; heart, guts, and flesh want to stretch out of me. And for a minute, I briefly understand why Pastor Joseph takes it upon himself to pressure the congregation to canvass every door on the surrounding blocks, to beg and strongarm the adjacent neighbourhood to attend the church, bless the church, save the church, and accept Jesus Christ as their Lord and Saviour, by all means necessary, coercing the freshest and most appealing among us as proof of His eternal love, pushing them to the doorsteps of despondent put-upon community, sending them up the high-rises, flouting "no-solicitations" signs hung up in corridors, as if that could convincing anyone to exchange one misery for another.

I can feel everyone's eyes on me as I traipse down the aisle. Eileen's jaw must be damn near grazing the floor. I can feel their incredulity as my hat slides off my face, as my hair frizzes out of its press, as the two undisciplined buttons pop off the blazers wrapped around my chest, as the breath and all the toxicity and judgement slips out of my panting mouth.

Meanwhile, Pastor Joseph seems pleased with himself.

"Yes, child," he utters, even though he is very much in my age cohort, while placing a moist hand first on my shoulder, and then on my forehead. I distinctly remember, sometime and place far away from here, making him cry in grade school, and watching him run back to his mama's house like a little rat.

"Yes, come home, Mattie," he whispers into the side of my face with that stale mouth that never once reached for the glass of water they left for him at the pulpit.

And my knees take to the faded carpet. My legs rub against the fibres, and I suddenly take notice of a run in my stockings that went from my shin to a point right above my knee. There are stains and crusty spots I can't identify on it, but, against all reason, I place my palms on them.

It is then that the choir leader guides the congregation into a rendition of "What a Fellowship." I can detect Eileen's screeching vibrato over everyone's voice. Its mocking tone. I can just imagine her triumph at seeing me here, like this, in this state of vulnerability. I know I am ridiculous. I want to get up, dust myself off, and indulge in a taxi ride to the cushioned safety of my apartment. And I almost do. The carpet smells musty. But here I am, crouched like a fool in the middle of a ramshackle church, with everybody looking on.

I wish I hadn't gotten up. I want to disappear and rematerialize in front of my television. I can't even bring myself to lift my face to look at anyone. My spirit is hovering somewhere above me, mocking me and ready to bolt at any moment. For a moment, I consider the possibility of playing dead, waiting for the service to close and the pews to empty so that I can skulk out of this place unseen. Oh, the mortification. But then I fixate on the swirling pattern of the carpet.

Pastor Joseph rubs the small of my back.

By then, my spirit is too far from his reach. Too far away to care. Doing as it will. On another wavelength. It is as if there is a line down my centre all the way beneath my feet, dripping down and boring a hole in the crust of the earth, about to swallow me into its hot core, into not nothingness but wholeness, to a level of warmth I've never felt before. And then, from my lips come words that had a shape and sound unknown to me, but all I know is that I have to say them right then and there lest they burn my chest and throat with their urgency. They tumble out of my mouth like hot coals and at my feet before this gathering of strangers, acquaintances, enemies, and their children.

I haven't felt this way since that moment years ago, when I'd buried a doll in the front yard, hoping to recover it later. When I returned, she was no longer there. There was a set of smooth round stones in her place. I complained to Auntie Shirley and she laughed at me and said, what did I expect? If you make an offering to the Earth, she'll swallow it.

Pastor Joseph grabs hold of my upper arm, making it as if he's steadying me as I walk down the platform steps.

"Easy there," he whispers in my ear, as I reach the last one.

He smiles from the corner of his mouth, and I see him truly for what he is. The town fool. The village jester in a misfitting pinstripe gray suit, hair coils semi-relaxed and brushed out to accentuate a wave pattern that suggests some Indian or Chinese blood.

It then occurs to me that I have braided kilometres and kilometres of heads in this stuffy room. Enough distance to fly someone back home. Here we are, a veritable reconstituted village. The expellees of every town of the tropics. Each thinks she constitutes another's auntie. Calcified, prying sistren, latching onto each other in a skeletal reconfiguration of many sleepy towns, a composite of the most opportunistic batch of distant relations who had the compulsion to leave what they had behind, which is to say everything and not much, only to enact a country in our heads.

And Pastor Joseph, the worst of the lot, has managed to clamber his way to the top of the pile, happy to direct the crowd toward some place known only to him, but which he claims can be interpreted plainly in the placed-by-the-Gideons Bibles that he redistributes.

I buck and bop like this for who knows how long, and it's not until the fresh air hits me in the church foyer and I catch sight of myself in a silver flower pot, that I regain my senses and become aware of my changed demeanour and feeling.

Just as I place my hair back into its chignon, Eileen saunters over to me with that vagabond in tow. She looks me up and down, all too interested.

"Looks like the spirit got into you."

"I suppose."

It's just like her, to rub things in my face, bring the obvious into evidence and distort it ever so slightly. I ought to take a hand to her face and smear the cakey makeup until it resembles an impressionist painting. But then, I also notice something else in her expression. A twitch in the corner of her eye, a twist of her lips that suggests some underlying disturbance. Could it be envy? I quickly banish that vision from my line of sight.

"Will you stay for potluck?"

No, I will not stay for potluck, and eat some stale reheated macaroni from this and that friend's of a cousin's sister's mother-in-law. Truth be told, I'd rather go to the nearest food court and enjoy my meal in front of complete strangers. At least then, I could enjoy the privacy of my anonymity.

As I wait outside for my bus, a few paces from the church entrance, I catch sight of a group of youngsters playing Double Dutch on the pavement of the church entrance.

Down by the riverside the green grass grows,
Where someone walks, some tiptoe.
She sings, she sings so sweet,

I get caught up in the rhythm of their games, my legs twitch with muscle memory. One of their mothers stumbles out of the church entrance and screeches at her child to stop mussing her hair and drags her away from the group of kids. Now, there's only two of them, missing a rope swinger. Just as they are about to disband, I traipse over to them and grab one end of it, to their bemusement.

Before any of them can protest, I swing the ropes and enchain:

She calls over to someone across the street.
Tea cakes, pancakes, everything you see,
Meet me in the hole at half past three.

Again, my tights slide down to my hips, the waistband is positively useless, rubbing against my midsection in a way that gets on my last nerve. None of the children pay attention or seem to care when I kick off my shoes and slide out of my damp pantyhose.

Loosed from them, the breeze wafts up and through my legs in a most liberating gust. For the first time that day, my bouboun breathes freely.

The Sims

In which Dom would rather not

ALWAYS AROUND 2AM, the carafes need changing. By then, the coffee has condensed into something rancid, more like silt than 100% Arabica. That marks the halfway point of a shift, which usually leaves me another four hours to finish.

Next, I unpack the depleted snacks. The nougat. The pork rinds. The bubblegum. I sling them on the shelves with the speed and precision of a casino dealer. Following that, I wipe the drink station and refill the French Vanilla mix, which runs out twice as fast as the other flavors. The Cappuccino mix, always the slowest to move, hardens into a cakey ring around the nozzle that I scrape away with my index fingernail.

With all my heart, I rebuke the bathroom. Reason alone to escape. It stinks of ammonia and rotting mop, no matter how much chemical warfare you wage on it. I let my focus wander while wiping specks of shit and piss from the surface of the toilet. I try not to think of each and every customer who has come and gone and left me with these offerings. I astral project myself to lovely parts of the universe while scrubbing and wiping, reaching for the industrial grade soap under the sink that I mix with several quarts of hot water. I run the mop across the floor, starting at the doorway, behind the carousel of maps and mini-flashlight key rings and then make my way along the front of the counter, in the path of the most stubborn dirt tracks and zigzag across every aisle until I swab myself back into the storage room.

With that done, I return to my post behind the counter and rest my elbows on its surface. I angle my body away from the security cam, so that the only footage it records is of my sweet ass.

And then there's the chime. It's muffled from where I sit now, but I can still sense it. The blur of impatient customers at the door. Those who know to wait usually stare through the glass with a glazed look while I buzz them in. New patrons usually try the door first, and then jiggle it until the door yields.

Some nod in my direction before leaving, without making eye contact. Others ignore me completely. I appreciate this kind of indifference. There is frankness, even clarity, in it. People think they have to extend tentacles of pleasantries to ease our transactions, but I shrug those off systematically.

I smile at them the way foxes grin—to signal defeat. My face, encircled in a mask of politeness. Beneath it is a mush of irritation and boredom. A tension between both layers.

Something about my perch at this counter makes me invisible, privy to so many conversations. For a time, I've been the wind you spit in. I was the ground you pissed into. I was the water that washed over everything, folding it into oblivion.

These are the gestures my body knows and wishes to forget. After several years of this routine, my muscles twitch toward these functions, always at odds with my desire to slacken every limb in my body. Same goes with my weary heart. In this line of work, you need to like people. And I like people, in that I like to watch them go around doing people stuff, but only from a safe distance.

*

Folks in New Stockholm come here to fight. It might start with a spontaneous commotion. Or long before, with a deep-rooted feud. People fight like they fall in love. Enthralled and needing to extract physical or psychic matter from each other.

Like those two in the parking lot. Always showing up here to argue. They wear flip flops, despite the weather. They're on another thaumaturgic vibration than everyone else. Overly enunciating yet somehow slurring their words like animatronic figures.

Usually, they're terse with each other. Trapped in whatever septic relationship dynamic they're brewing. Seeking a decor for their mise-en-scène.

If I were directing their lovers' quarrels, I would nix the narrative realist setup, apply a good smear of Vaseline on the lens. Golden hour. Edge of a coastal bluff. Cracked red earth. Swelling violins. Wind machine cranked up to the max. Close up on their faces.

"Fuck you."

"Fuck *you*."

Sometimes their aggression splatters over bystanders, like a slushie thrown at the counter. It's enough to make you want to build a swimming pool around them without an exit ladder. Watch them wade in it until they learn to love each other again.

*

You would think that management would express concern about my whereabouts on the first day I skip my shift, but no, they don't even raise a brow. It's like they expect me not to be here, like there is a maximum number of shifts they figured I would show up to work. They simply call Selly in earlier, they splice time and cut out the tape of my absence, and forget about me entirely.

I can always tell when Selly pulls into the parking lot. Her wheels screech. Rumple-faced, she nods hello as she prepares the till. Preoccupied with not messing up the count, I nod back without taking my eyes off her stacks for more than a second. She steps into the booth and rearranges the countertop to her liking. Enough elbow space to collapse her upper body on it.

In my head, I replay our most impassioned conversations.

"Anything new?"

"Nope."

"Cool."

*

An amber glow filters through the insulation. Dawn already. I watch for this exact moment of the day, when the parking lot buzzes with the morning crowd. The everloving chime. It will be another two hours before I get some shut eye.

Circadian rhythm's all messed up. When I can't sleep, I fix myself a bowl of Corn Flakes mixed with Cheerios and 2% milk. While writhing on my mat, I balance the bowl and splash a bit of milk on the blanket I dragged up here.

My relationship with the sun has changed. More of an abstraction than an intolerable thing that would hit me in the face when I emerged from my shift every day.

What if that big ball of gas decided to boil over and spew its contents into outer space? Imagine the devastation. We're due for another Carrington Event. Any day now, our technological infrastructure will come crashing down on our heads.

Which represents an opportunity, of course. With one whip of a solar flare, there'd be a window of time to run interference on so many systems. The prison labour camps. The death farms. The for-profit end-of-life asylums. I can already picture the formerly incarcerated emerging from their fences, buildings, and cages. Blinking up at the sun with relief.

*

I can feel the whisper of a shadow of a suggestion of a cavity in one of my left molars. When I bite into a spoonful of Cheerio-flecked Corn Flakes, the hollowness reverberates in my skull. How can such a small hole send my nerves into a frenzy? Wish I could reach into the void and muffle the ache. I'm already imagining a scenario in which I would extract the tooth using a string connected to one of the wood beams on the unfinished wall. Hope it's solid.

In the meantime, I'm becoming more aware of the strained relationship between my neck and shoulders. What could have provoked such chaos between them? They refuse to see each other as one. My new roommate, a little gray attic mouse, has kindly offered to scamper up and down my upper back, the closest you can get to a lymphatic massage.

*

I wish I'd brought my Sims with me. They used to distract me from my ailments, physical and emotional. There's nothing like a Sims expansion pack to bring the gameplay to the next level and unlock features that will treat them to an enhanced quality of life. One where most of your needs are met. Unlike the hostile installations—bench separators, window ledge spikes, neverending construction—that furnish our everyday lives in New Stockholm. Starting with the basics–the lavish bathrooms, kitchens, living rooms. But there's no way I'm enforcing nuclear family units. It's two dozen adults per pod, minimum. I mean, Sims just get it. They don't have thousands of years of toxic programming to restrain them into robotic lives or hinder them from wandering into the kitchen for some woo-hoo time in full sight of each other. Those wonderful beings take everything in stride. You can design them an underground bunker, a sex room, a cat wearing a tuxedo, and they'll have themselves an excellent time.

I prefer to engage with New Stockholm as a concept rather than an embodied reality. Why exhaust myself when I can experience the thing virtually. I mean, how intentional was its design, really? You mean to tell me I have to reckon with the mess made by a handful of misguided white guys, the aftermath of which their descendants still enjoy all while pleading innocence? Nah, I'll sit this one out. I mean, every aspect of this place exudes weaponized incompetence. From the aggressively anti-human highway grid, to the overly centralized food supply, to the limited game mechanics.

And don't get me started on its institutions. Guess how long it takes to send a rigged PDF to the admin at Defense Construction Incorporated and wait for them to wheel in the Trojan? After a mere four hours, I was already having a field day perusing their contact list, their security log sheet, and shared inboxes. How mediocre a company can reveal itself to be on the inside. Scotched together by a website and a mandate. Dig deeper and it's high employee turnover, porn addictions, and sexual harassment lawsuits waiting to happen.

Checked in on the infamous Doudou Laguerre's digital whereabouts too, and it was like pushing a cardboard wall. Even for a minor-league outlaw, it's a bit surprising that he'd go with Password1!. No complaints on my end though. It's always a pleasure to build a vision of someone through their inbox. In this case: media requests. Black Hebrew Israelite newsletters, pricey loc shampoo. Dude is a well-coiffed idealogue. I'd join his crew if it weren't for my weak ankles. Seems a bit athletic, what they do. Plus, I don't have the adrenal capacity.

Alas, my body is a bundle of frayed nerves. And still, this is the calmest my nervous system has been in ages. Since autonomously sheltering in place, the most excitement I've felt was when the gray attic mouse nibbled at my pinky toe the other night. Little guy went on about how he mistook it for a stuffed olive and didn't realize it was attached to me. As if.

*

My father used to tell me, "Life isn't a game, Dom. You have to work for what you want." Who said games weren't work? Watch me play, Daddy.

Here's a sport I like: Follow-the-dime. I hate to imagine where I would be today had it not slipped out of my pocket and rolled through the storage room and hit the wall with a hollow thoink! connected to a fake wall that led to a trap door that led to an attic. Who knew I could find my way to the back of the stock room, climb the ladder and lie down in the attic above the store. I could stack a bunch of chips and dip and red Gatorade, enough to last me a couple of weeks, until I needed some again.

Here's another one I enjoy: pocket-Sprint. I may have a direct line of sight on the parking lot through the clerestory window, but it's a wonder of nature, skill and intent that I manage to shorten the register up when Selly and the other night shift employees share a smoke out front before switching guards, convinced that they've left an empty store behind them. This gives me time to come down, stretch for a bit, stock up on grub, empty my piss pot, and ensure that I can do this for a bit longer. Sometimes, just for kicks, I swipe out a few coins from the leave-a-penny-take-a-penny, like Selly does when she assumes no one is looking. Just tips it over the counter, picks it off the floor, and returns it empty. I wonder what she's saving up for? Definitely not shoes, judging by the brand she wears—Adibas, with the second d reversed in a way that confuses my dyslexic ass.

And my favorite game of all: Fill-in-the-Blanks. I'm designing the future as I go. With the cash I'll save, I figure I could probably get myself a bus ticket out of New Stockholm, head to the woods, find access to shelter and clean water, plant fruit trees, make friends with all the woodland creatures, invite my friends, throw some parties, and then, depending on the mood, spend my days painting the landscape with homemade pigments or carving whimsical little figures into soapstone, while simultaneously working to heal my body and mind, improve my flexibility, tend to my joint pain and trauma, and, sure, from that point on, maybe someday in the midst of this Edenic niche, a series of ravishing and kindhearted strangers would emerge from the woods, seeking companionship or sex or both or none, and with time, some of us may have babies that would play with the pups, the cubs, the kits, and all of us would live out the rest of our days in absolute peace, letting our teeth grow strong and resilient, picking and eating ripened apples and mangos off the trees that our bodies would someday fertilize in a most round and satisfying life cycle.

Yes, I could raise strong and resilient-toothed children on tree-ripened fruit, if I just sit here in this store for a little longer and lean into the silence, into the narrowness of the space, memorize the gurgles and trickles of the plumbing and enjoy the silence between customers. That bell, it rings without any logic. There's no telling when and how long the intervals last. Irregular as wind whistling through trees. Sometimes, there are rattles in quick succession, as if the world makes sense, as if there's a knot of consciousness that unties itself and leads five to six customers to fill up their tanks or pick up an energy drink. Otherwise, it's just random, that ding, followed by the patter of footsteps or mumbles of small talk, the air currents of my day.

Uh huh, one day, I'll come down the ladder once more and skim the cash register for the last time, and take off for the closest patch of woods. Until then, I'll be Selly's clandestine companion.

*

But I'm not overly worried about the next steps. Even though my back has joined the feud between my neck and shoulders, there is lots to enjoy inside my nook. I swiped a few titles from the so-so collection of paperbacks in the case near the register. These Harlequins aren't half-bad once you ignore the theatrics and the overuse of suggestive words like "hoist."

How I miss my old roommate. Her stacks of dirty bowls. That donkey laugh of hers. Those beads that got everywhere. Wish I could go back to the apartment and clear the air. Maybe grab a couple of proper sci-fi erotica novels on my way out, except that I can't jeopardize what I have here. I'm playing the long game.

Yet here I am. Just when I should be wiping that toilet, I'm terminally horny and playing dead in the attic, ignoring the chime and wondering if Selly is starting to intuit my presence. It wouldn't be on account of my indiscretions, such as those coughing fits that I choke down. I've been more than circumspect. I keep my movements to a minimum and slink around smoothly like a serpent. I only chew my food when she does, and my swallows of red Gatorade mirror hers. Our digestion is practically synchronized. I only need to crouch over the piss pot when she's making her way to the bathroom.

Rather, I wonder if she can sense my particular vibe. The earth's natural frequency is 7.83 hertz. Having been up here for a little over three weeks, I must be vibrating out of whack. You can feel these things, sight unseen.

My meditation ritual must help. First, I visualize myself as a garden bed, filled with rich peaty soil, into which I psychically plant seeds of faith, hope, and abundance. Then, I picture a graceful horse wandering over my garden self, leaving a trail of fresh shit to fertilize me. Next, I imagine the sun and rain that feed my seedlings and see them to maturity, a stage of lushness that leads to an abundant harvest followed by winter. I repeat the cycle all over again, until I lull myself back into a state of serenity or fall asleep. Just as I almost nod off, the couple in the parking lot returns. They're unusually silent this time. She hums a tune lightly and cradles a bag of tortilla chips in her arms as if it's an infant. Ever so gently, he takes it from her and pulls her into a side hug.

I guess I'll just spend time recreating this visualization or other spicier storylines in my head. It's fine, as long as there's silence, especially at night when the stream of customers slows down, when I can hear that hum of the refrigerators, the hiss of the heating, and the squeak of the hot dog spit. If I'm going to be lying here, I might as well devote some time to visualizing tits. Juicy responsive titties attached to someone I care about.

Or taking in the sights. When I crane my neck to the east wall, the bits of insulation call to mind pink cumulonimbus clouds. Any minute now, they're about to rain rose-hued glitter on my head.

Don't get me wrong, this absolute hell is also a sweet kind of withdrawal, as if all this life has culminated into an alternate reality. No frills. Just another turn of the screw, counterclockwise, lefty loosey, dismantling the machine.

The little gray attic mouse thinks I should show more gratitude. Mind you, he's been at it a lot longer than me, so he doesn't have much patience for my human antics. Proportionately, that is. There's the delicate matter of his shorter life span. About two years, if he's lucky. Better to make the best of it. Dude makes a good point. For one, I finally have time to contemplate the intricacies of a mango. How much more sensual can a shape be—a titillating comma-like curve. Overwhelming sweetness layered over a pop of tartness. I peel them by biting into the skin.

My vision is clouded with sparkles, forcing my pupils shut. It's the inverse of stargazing. Sometimes you have no choice but to let your eyes roll to the back of your head and explore the many layers of sensation that exist within.

*

The tooth pain has officially escalated. Shout-out to the little gray attic mouse for offering me a thimble of medicine while squeaking consoling thoughts.

Sometimes I think I've left a part of myself behind the counter. A ghost, a simulacrum of my full self. What a basic existence! I can't imagine what I have in common with that groveling yokel, that cog in the wheel of this storefront. The way they smile at customers. The way that smile lingers on their lips well after the customer has left, as they stand behind that counter in front of cigarette boxes labeled with macro photos of busted larynxes and skin diseases. Poor form. To unconsciously appease the regulars, they hum along to the muzak played on the radio.

By studying this robotic doppelganger, I've concluded that I can convince myself of my own satisfaction. Not happiness, mind you. Not wisdom either, but satisfaction, the minimum of what a life requires, just by not placing a physical or spiritual object between yourself and your routine, that thing you are compelled to do everyday.

If there was a god, I would worship these wooden beams, insulation, and scaffolding that stand between me and that life, that remind me of my humanity and bring me back to a primal state, the fetal position. So far, this is my best work, and I don't intend to surpass myself. If there is a god, and I am said god, trust that I would create the most sensible universe imaginable. Just wait. Until then, I continue to chew through the pain and slurp the last sweet dregs of cereal milk.

Rough Cut

In which Maya encounters a good thing and a bad thing

THIS IS BULLSHIT. It won't work. The editor doesn't get it.

The cuts are way too jumpy. Much too frenetic. They lack aeration, finesse. What a disaster. If only I could travel back in time to that moment and re-shoot the entire sequence. That, or Zeynab needs to fire Nick, her editor.

If only Nick-the-Editor had been there, he would know what to do with the shot that establishes the remoteness of the shore, where a flock of seagulls, cawing offscreen, swoops down and enters the frame, suggestive of the macabre. And then another tighter shot in which the early evening sun filters through the overcast sky and back-lights the rocky beach, exaggerating its grainy texture, just before a break in the clouds lets through a string of sun rays that radiates a solar flare.

Fucking Nick. What he's done–it doesn't add up. You can't just open on a corpse, or an activist dude the cops only freshly IDed. You have to build your way in. You have to contextualize it–him. Doudou Laguerre. Cipher Falls' very own Robin Hood. You must prime the viewer's gaze to appreciate who they're taking in. To sense his weight. To feel his loss. Otherwise, you're relying on shock value. What he's done–it verges on the pornographic.

It's really a pity because this scene has the power to elevate this film from mere reportage to the ineffable. Speaking of which, Zeynab seems blasé in the face of these decisions. Positively checked out. In fact, she suggested we should cut the sequence entirely, which, what the hell. I swear, she's dedicated to sabotaging this project.

But hey, it's not up to me. That much is clear, by the way the editor recoiled when Zeynab introduced me as the camera operator. As if she'd dragged the actual corpse into the editing suite. Sure, I'm the legs, the arms, the eye. Never the brain. I knew I shouldn't have come. Worst of all, you can barely talk, let alone sip a coffee in peace in the editing suite at the Film Commission. Goddamn Nick took one look at my coffee and bag of chips and sent me packing right out of there to finish it in the hallway. As if a few salt and vinegar chips could get into the ridges and compromise the workstation. State-of-the-art shit right there. How many of our fucking tax dollars are funding this? I did the calculations. Maybe 15 people a year get to use this shit, at most. I consider confiscating a piece of equipment, but think against it when I notice the surveillance camera in the corner of the room. I guess their business plan is to let this equipment depreciate and upgrade it with the next federal budget allocation.

It's a different game at this level. Let me tell you, I've dragged my kit through thick and thin, and every rugged corner of the city, from its crooked alleyways to congested metro stations, on my way to every gig imaginable.

It's just as well that Zeynab's been calling me at all hours of the night over the past months and has finally invited me into the editing suite to view the first cut. I could get used to this, even though it kills me to see my beautiful shots rendered into her unintelligible sequences and scenes. I get it. She's got a schtick. A well-worn gimmick that she trots out at every juncture. That is, of using the ephemera of life as evidence of the thing itself. Come on, that's just getting old.

To me, it comes off as a convenient way of circumventing any responsibility to engage with reality. I'm sorry, but she can't just sit back and let the people finance her personal healing quest. She's accountable for the discourse she puts out in the world, and she could very well ignore that fact, but somewhere down the line, her work ceases to belong to her and enters the public domain. Otherwise, the whole exercise becomes an elitist circle-jerk. There's no way around it.

Yes, she's vibing on our dime. Since Zeynab is a part of the privileged rigged lottery-winning minority of people who get their work funded, the onus is on her to do this work. Hey, you don't work at the post office just so that you can do a deep dive into your family trauma. No, you get your ass out there and deliver the mail, pronto. There's a public conversation she wants to start, and she can't be making work as an extension of her ego. But what is she, if not all ego? Look at her, with that retreating posture, those twitchy artist's hands, that carefully styled outfit. She sickens me in that she is everything I'm not. And her adoring following is mostly white, whether she acknowledges it or not.

It makes me sick, the way the Film Commission staff fawn over Zeynab, but I can appreciate that it probably stems from the manner she commands their respect, instills fear. The way those two producers, Tweedledee and Tweedledum look at her, like she's the second coming of the Black Madonna, with their cheshire grins, asking if she wants a water bottle or another espresso. The same Nick-the-Editor who berated me for bringing in chips casually asked her if she wanted to order some take-out. I mean, come on!

I would venture to say that what we have so far is passable. Months after filming grim landscapes and a spate of interviews, I can see the substance forming. But that's where my hope stops. She has no plan. No ambition. She seems to prefer to take the passive route of studying the footage indefinitely before making any decisions.

I still have no idea why Zeynab calls me into these sessions. Probably as a foil. Everyone wants a sidekick, some drooling Igor to flip the giant switch. It's like I'm her Chewbacca, emitting a RRWWWGG every so often, just to remind everyone I'm there. Maybe she just likes the friction of our interactions. She gets a gleam in her eye whenever I open my mouth and make Nick squirm. And goodness knows, I'll give him hell. Overpaid ass. But I'm not sure she herself is ready to hear what I really think. I would jump at the chance to bring this film to the next level, open up important questions around DCI's involvement in the suspicious death of a beloved community member who was openly known to sabotage their construction project, even though they've refused to comment on Laguerre's mysterious death. He was too dangerous, is what. For chrissake, she could bring down the whole establishment and have an actual impact, but there she is, playing at research-creation.

My stomach grumbles.

"Shhhh."

Zeynab places her chin in her hands and then rubs her temples. I wait for it. Seven months have gone by and I can always tell when she's about to drop a new idea. She's like a cash cow of concepts, this one.

"Wait a minute. Superimpose all the audio."

Nick-the-Editor obliges.

There are 25 interviews, some pre-interviews, all with individuals who've had an encounter with Doudou, DCI, the New Stockholm Development Board or all three. Most of their testimonies align to point to the obvious; being expropriated from your home fucking sucks. But what's peculiar is the fact that each one of them systematically concludes with a segment after which Zeynab probes them, either verbally or with those arresting eyes of hers, in a way that provokes an unexpected display of emotion or dismantles the facade they show up with to the interview. Or perhaps it's that she catches them with the last bit of resolve they had to spare, combined with the relief of ending the seance at which point they let out a sigh, maybe loosen their shoulders, slacken their jaws, or soften their eyes, which has the potential, with her careful nudging, to turn into full-bodied sobs that should have been released years ago.

That is, according to Zeynab, where the real interview starts. Presently, just the audio is playing, and there is a sound of the supernatural, guttural order, a deep down that emanates from the speakers. Like the sound of an opening fridge on a hot day. Quite subtle. Jesus Christ, she's decided to scrap all of the visual content of the interview and layer the audio over images of the landscape. And somehow it works. My god, it works.

When Tweedledee and Tweedledum are called into the editing suite, they look at us with scepticism.

"What do you have for us?"

"You should remember that this doesn't have to be the final montage. We could also circulate and come back to this rough cut later…"

Zeynab interrupts him by clicking the playback button.

And the sound that rings out. That sound, that glorious sound. It's loud. It's vibrant. It's resonant. It's strangely affecting? Tweedledum's knees appear to buckle under him, and he crumbles to the floor, shocked at his own display of emotion.

As for Tweedledum, he drops his takeout tray, what might be lasagna, judging from the crimson splotch on the tile. As her colleague scrambles to pick up the mess, Tweedle-dee sidesteps the fragrant pile and extends her arms toward Zeynab.

"You… prodigy!" she says, gaping as usual.

"Yeah, you've created a beautiful filmic object here," echoes Tweedledum, picking a limp noodle off the floor. Definitely lasagna.

Wow. What a way to say nothing at all. They need to get the fuck out of here with their corporate art jargon. But I say nothing. I leave it to Zeynab to take care of the interfacing. She's got this way around it, where she does very little, just sort of asserts herself through mannerisms. Sometimes when I look over, she looks absent, like there's no one home.

When everyone leaves, it's just the two of us in the silence of the room. She turns to me.

"You don't like it?" asks Zeynab.

"Um okay, well, do what you want, obviously. It's your film. It's not my place at all to comment. But then again, you do keep calling me in to see the footage. You do ask me what I think, and so I might as well remind you about all that time we spent shooting and what that meant, and I would just hope that you would remember to honor it when working toward the picture lock."

There she is, eyes glazing over. She's just asked me a question and yet isn't interested in hearing an honest answer. Well, fuck it, then. I turn to leave. I've got a long night ahead. Might as well hit the road.

"Have you eaten yet?"

"Uh, maybe. But I'm going to a thing."

I look at her, and think about the bus, the long transfers, the last grubby station, and the sketchy overworked people and Chekhov who's probably waiting for me impatiently.

She gives me such bourgie vibes, I'm almost ashamed to admit that I intend to pass by one of Ioannis's gigs downtown, which he assured me had a good spread and free-flowing wine. There's no way I'm missing out on that.

"What thing?"

"A conference."

"Which one?"

"Something about the performing arts."

"The performance studies conference?"

"Yeah, that's the one."

"Oh, a friend of mine is organising that. What if I joined you?"

"Um, I guess so. Why not."

Now this is weird. I always figured she went back to her cryogenic tube at the end of the day.

When we finally pack up to leave the building, which is no small feat, given the extensive security protocol, I realise that it's much colder outside than I'd expected.

There's always an overcast sky over New Stockholm at this time of year that gives it a pinkish hue at sunset. It might seem appealing, but that's just pollutants and aerosols. This city's been rendered so many times by wannabe street photographers and tourists, it exists as a postcard in people's minds. The real deal feels like carbon monoxide poisoning. In which you just sit there comfortably, entrenched in your blissful confusion, unaware of the fact that you're chilling in a deathtrap. I can't trust anyone who snaps selfies on the street. Way to document your own slow demise, buddy. There are two types of citydwellers, those who let their eyes wander and drink in the sights and those who dodge bubblegum and spit on the sidewalk.

Zeynab is definitely one of the latter. She seems weirdly at odds with the world when you see her on the street. The way she stops and starts every couple of steps, and how she pauses talking to look up, as if the sky is falling. Kind of endearing, I guess.

As soon as we reach New Stockholm University, I dial Ioannis's number so that he can get us in. Shit goes right to voicemail. When we approach the registration table, the volunteer eyes me with disinterest and flashes a polite smile my way, but as soon as they turn to Zeynab, their smile widens with recognition.

"Hey girl! How've you been?"

"Oh, you know. Doing life, as usual."

"Totally. Are you coming to Laurie's dinner next week? There's this sound designer from out of town that she'd really like to put you in touch with."

"Oh?"

"Yeah, her shit is unbelievable. She works with water and sound waves, really funky stuff. I swear you've never heard anything like it."

"Oh!"

Without asking, she hands us each a packet and name tags and sends us on our way.

The moment we drift into the atrium, I scan the crowd, out of habit. It's a mix of NSU students, queers, and other community members. You have the practitioners, at the ready with their business cards and social media handles, a bit scrappy and out of place in the setting, but they took a day off to breathe this rarified air, making the most of it, busy striking a conversation with whoever looks open enough to tolerate a good old rant about the vagaries of grassroots work. You have the academic stars and their hardwon pedigree, their tactical skill, the air of hunger that trails alongside them. You can practically inhale the thick clouds of microaggressions that fuel their quests for authority. And there's no forgetting the tastemakers, the artists who are lightyears ahead of everyone and manage to make a living off vibes alone, in addition to maybe some sort of covert support, perhaps a grant here, a good connection there, that keeps them breathing and worldbuilding. And then you have the rest. The loners, the workshop-hoppers, the intellectual drifters, the wandering souls who haunt the NSU campus, hoping to absorb social, institutional, and financial capital by osmosis, always willing to provide an audience, ready to clap and gawk on cue.

But where's the cafeteria? If I don't eat soon, I'll blow this fucking place up.

Zeynab starts making conversation with someone else that she just casually knows. There she goes, flitting about with her impeccable eyeliner, as people turn to her and dive into magnificent personal narratives that they urgently need her to know. Turns out that this one is a goddess of networking, a juggler of social circles who commands any room she walks into. I watch in awe as she translates her aloof exterior into a magnetic field. She doesn't even have to say anything of value. In conversation, she has this way of saying "Oh?" that hits the right note of skepticism and curiosity and gets people to launch into further detail. Impressive. I could never pull it off in the same way. I would just sound ignorant. Not nearly interdisciplinary or conceptual enough.

While Zeynab discusses, I storm off and do another round of the atrium. Near the entrance of the main conference room, I run into Ioannis, who seems zonked out of his mind, toggling between his three cameras, barking orders at his new assistant.

"Hey man, sorry I missed your call. How've you been?"

"Not bad, dude."

"You look good."

"Yeah, you know. Surviving."

"Still working with Zeynab?"

"Yeah."

"Well, I look forward to seeing what y'all come out with."

"Thanks, man."

"Alright, I'll see you later."

"Hey wait… You wouldn't happen to have anything for me?"

His eyes suddenly light up with understanding. He fishes through his pockets, raises a hand, and slaps four food and drink vouchers into my hand.

"Thanks, man. I owe you one."

"No problem, bro."

I moonwalk away from him and electric slide to the cafeteria. When she notices me passing by, Zeynab, cool as hell, cuts short a conversation and follows me out of the atrium and down the hallway. I'm guessing the spread should be top-notch, judging by the prestige of the school. This campus is full of loot hiding in plain sight. Free condoms. Slave trader monuments. Last summer, I even managed to find an almost brand new computer monitor in front of one of the dorms. Probably belonged to some international students who usually junk their good wares in street corners at the end of their last semester. I have a reminder in my calendar to come by here every year.

So they've gone with a tapas menu. Honestly, I would have preferred a meal with more inherent volume, but I make it work by loading my plate as much as I can. It's an impractical selection, but at least there's variety. Gooey things. Crunchy stuff. Everything in between. In the first round at the buffet line, I try everything once to establish my preference, and then load my favorites onto my plate the second time around, disregarding the concerned stares from the cafeteria staff. On my way out, I balance two cups of wine in one hand and make sure to pocket as many giant cookies as my jacket can hold.

Zeynab and I take our heaping plates into one of the sessions. I don't quite catch the topic of this one, but it's packed with attendees who lap up every word of a Q&A between a white moderator who looks like they're trying their hardest to extract discourse from an artist who is wearing a glittery bodysuit and a full-face of rainbow makeup, heavy on contour, light on restraint, looking like an extra from *The Lion King*. As they respond to the line of questions, they seem caught somewhere between boredom and outrage at being quizzed by an academic.

Meanwhile, I go hard on the spread, eating from both my plate and Zeynab's, leaving no stuffed olive unsucked while trying to follow the discussion.

"And how would you categorize your art practice?"

"Well, first of all, categorization is a form of violence. Secondly, art might be a misnomer here. I resist that label because of its emphasis on output. The point, for me at least, is not the final outcome. And if you're brave, it's about the process of making things together."

"But what does Ouroboros work toward? You said you make things together?"

"Yes, ineffable things."

"Such as...?"

"Pleasure."

"Pleasure?"

"Yes, we get together, and produce it."

"Could you expand on this a bit for us?"

"Yes, sure. There's a richness that emerges when multiple people delve into action at once. But, of course, that can get a little chaotic. The way we mitigate that is by collectively brainstorming and agreeing on a set of boundaries. It could be a line in the sand. Or pylons. Or a rope. Sometimes it's a conceptual limit. Such as, 'no hands,' 'no eye contact,' or 'only words.' It could be all of the above. And then we get right to it. Usually, the game—because it is a game, isn't it —organizes itself. It's like putting one word after the other, then one sentence after the other, one after the other, until the rules just establish themselves."

"How so?"

"Take last month, for example. Someone, a member of the collective, was initiating, and she was set on doing something with her voice. I believe she'd best explain this herself, but what I could gather from her gesture was that she was ululating in a variety of patterns, like HIGH-LOW-HIGH-LOW-HIGH-LOW or even HIGH-LOW-LOW-HIGHER-HIGHEST-HIGH-LOW-LOW-LOWER and inviting everyone else to join her until everyone was interpreting it, and then she'd switch it up in ways that were unexpected to glean as much interest as possible. And then all of sudden, I'm not sure who started it, but then someone else came out of nowhere and added movement to the sound, which is a pretty obvious way to go, if I'm honest, but still, no one had thought about it until that moment, and before you knew it, everyone was ululating and undulating simultaneously, but in like, different ways. We even had people adding sound variations, like glottal stops and clapping, and that was chill."

"And how long did it go on like this?"

"That's not necessarily something we focus on. Linear time. But to engage with the spirit of your question: We could have continued all night, into the next day. Nobody was stopping, and I had to put out some snacks and instruct people to tap out to eat or drink because of the choking hazard, but I can tell you that some people even brought the rhythm to the toilet. There was spillage everywhere in the loft. It had a choral effect, like what you'd expect to see inside a beehive or a literal wormhole if you look under the right rock. Just a writhing ball of life. Anyway, the neighbours shut that down pretty fast."

"Is this usually how the games go?"

"Depends on the medium. There's something about the substance you're dealing with that dictates the form. Painting is pretty mild. It takes a kind of quiet to render lines. Some other media are naturally livelier. Sex, for instance—"

"Sex?"

"Yes, and it's generally pretty complex to manage, but the trick is to set up the right parameters, boundaries, whatever you wanna call them. And towels."

"Hold on, you mean that your collective organizes sex parties?"

"Sure, but I'd rather tell you about it from the frame of process rather than outcome. You see, when you're having sex with an agenda, it tends to get in the way of itself. Whether you're trying to consolidate a romantic or domestic relationship or trying for a baby, all these forms of sex are a bit, let's say that they reduce the act to a form of service or transaction, or consumption. Notice that "consummation" is the term for the act in a legal-marital context. What if instead we deconstructed sex and questioned its form? When does it start? Where does it end? For humans to work together is the most powerful technology."

"Indeed."

"For humans to work together," she repeats, "is the most powerful technology."

"Wow, well, thanks for this. For those who are just joining us, Tamika has kindly offered to lead us in a form of prayer, what she calls an incantation to the...."

Oof. Time to jet. I've had my fill. We have feasted throughout most of the session. Well, I did. Zeynab mainly picked at her plate one minute, focusing on the speaker the next, zoning out and looking like a spectre of herself. She barely ate. I turn to her and make the universal sign for "let's get the hell outta here."

We sidle out of the auditorium toward the exit. In the atrium, which has cleared out significantly, one of her organizer friends hands us a leftover bottle of red. We crack it open on a bench.

My first sip sinks deep into my belly, easing a tension that was there unbeknownst to me. For the first time in a while, I loosen my shoulders and let out a deep sigh like a growl. Zeynab stares at a point ahead of her, with an expression I've rarely seen on her face. Eyes dull and facial muscles slackened like she's asleep or entranced. She snaps out of it and puts on her prim little mask again when she notices me looking at her.

"Did you notice the bats?"

"Whatta?"

"Look up."

And there they are, four of those furry guys hanging from the ceiling, more snuggly than you'd imagine. Quite serene, actually. One of them shivers and flaps its wings gently and then simmers down again. Sweet baby.

That's when I remember Chekhov. Damn, it's already half past midnight. Only seven minutes until the last bus, which would make me late to the subsequent connecting buses. And trust, at the rate she's paying me, you would think I could afford a ride home, but you try cultivating disposable income when you're still paying the interest off your student loans from art school. At this rate, I'll still be filling up on free institutional food at age 70, just for the privilege of fussing over a synopsis that no one will ever read. My shoulders start to rise again, back to their usual stressed position, and I take a big nervous swig out of the bottle of red. She leans into me.

"What's up?"

"Missed the last bus. I'm fucked, man."

"You can crash at mine."

"Really?"

"No worries."

"Nah, it's cool. I could ask my friend Ioannis for a lift if he's still around."

"No, I insist."

"Are you sure it's not a bother?"

"Pretty sure."

"Well then, I mean, thanks? That would be such a life-saver."

And then there's an awkward silence during which she holds my gaze without saying a word, and I can't stand it so I reach into my pocket and throw one of my giant cookies at her, just to see how crushed pastry would interact with her insufferably captivating face, and then she snatches the bottle out of my hand and splashes me on the chest and suddenly, we're laughing uncontrollably, cackling loudly, until we get asked to leave by a security guard. By the time we meander out of the atrium and off the university campus, the damp air culminates into a light drizzle.

*

We march in silence all the way back to her place.

Which is a whole mess. Not in the hygienic sense, but in that the layout is anarchic. Not a piece of furniture in sight. Not even a shelf or tabletop. Just a blood red oriental rug with a trippy concentric pattern, wall-to-wall mirrors, as in a dance studio, and books propped up in rambling piles against the walls, forming a ledge. Everything low to the ground, unmoored from any semblance of structure. Other than this, a massive collection of military trenches and random accessories splayed out in a free-floating space.

It's all the more evident to me that I've been dealing with a haphazard thinker all along. Just running on impressions and good luck.

Intuitively, I guess that the cluster of notebooks, empty mugs, and a laptop serves as her office space." It has a monastic vibe.

Adjacent to her workspace is what I take for her bed, from the stuffed animal and pillows. And the books. Her collection runs from old horror-film criticism magazines to generic encyclopedias. Probably filler to create the impression of volume. Right away, I zero in on the goods.

"*Bitch Planet!* I love these!"

She gives me a look like she's trying to play it cool, but I see a smidge of pride in her face.

"Fun, right?"

"Yeah, do you want some tea?"

While she fills the kettle, I flip through one of the issues.

She brings back the tea, crouches into her workspace, and unravels her hijab and unbinds her braids, all without using her hands. Practiced gestures. I join her on the rug, which feels sumptuous as sin.

"Girl, is this wool?"

"Silk."

"The fuck? I could die right here."

I run a hand on the velvety carpet fibers and catch sight of our reflection in one of the mirrors. We look like the subjects of a mango diaspora poem. An intimate foray into mirrored desire. Something, something, ocean metaphor. Look at me. All the soft gushy parts of me that secretly want to lie back and surrender to the crushing weight of joy get transmuted into the urge to conceptualize a photo essay. I could preface the piece with a statement about sleepovers as a radical act of care, and expound on how they subvert the heteronormative domestic sphere. The captions would consist of transcriptions of phrases found around her studio. 100% Organic Shea butter. *The Black Unicorn. Sula.* It's not like me to reduce someone to their consumption habits, but there's something in the sum of it all that signals that we might have actually lived through similar comings of ages.

"So what did you really think of the rough cut?" She's looking at me like she wants to drill into my brain and retrieve the goods.

"I mean, it's definitely doing something, but have you thought about the ethics of revealing the, you know, the whole..."

"You mean the corpse?"

"Well, yeah, the body. For one, have you talked to his family and friends?"

She arches an eyebrow, and I brace myself for the blowback. But then she reaches over and gathers my hands in hers, a contact that makes me flinch, and then relax, and then flinch again when she squeezes them.

"First of all, I'm horrified that I hadn't thought of this before. Also, I can tell that it took you a lot of courage to give me this feedback. That is a lovely recommendation, and I appreciate your sensitivity."

What's left of my breath escapes through my ears. Is this what it's like for someone to zero in on you through a viewfinder? To be seen? Naked and vulnerable. I'm starting to understand her gravitational pull. She's like a well-built camera. Complex mechanism but you just want to be in her line of sight. Or seeing through her. I can't remember the last time my body felt so at ease. My shoulders have melted down to a natural position, broken free from their usual squareness. Just like that, I'm seeing today's editing session in a brand new light. As a push and pull, a collective process. This is bliss. Perfection, even. Well, nothing is perfect—conflict is an essential part of the human experience. But I've just never felt this soothed.

What the fuck is in this tea? It's all becoming clear to me. We were placed on each other's paths to learn from each other. I from her, and she from me. We may disagree on stuff, but we have so much to say to each other, work on together, given that we occupy so much of the same common ground, speak the same language.

"So do you have any more feedback for me?"

"Yes. Give me this rug."

"Oh yeah?"

"Yeah, it'll probably bring the film to another level."

She chuckles and kisses my hands softly, which feels like a weirdly chivalrous move. And yet my stomach flutters. I retrieve my hands and fold them in my lap. Where to go from here? I hadn't counted on her being this personable. It's almost easier to interact with her aloof persona. So we hang there and look at each other, suspended in an ellipsis.

It occurs to me that we are a pair of quotation marks strewn on the page of her apartment floor. That'd be a good line for the photo essay. A bit pompous, but it works. She and I. We have work to do. Serious fish to fry. I can picture our children. Film-babies. With her ears. My mouth. Growing a legacy. Taking the world by storm. Creating whole new structures. With her tits. My mouth.

She's methodical, come to think of it. Keeps a tight record of the places on my body that respond to her touch, measures their intensity, revisits them, cross-examines them with the utmost care. Remembers to check in the deeper into the process we delve, unrelenting, thorough. Gives me space to hear back my own words, my voice. Probes every now and then and encourages me to challenge my limits.

She's thorough, even. By the end of it, before I even realize it, I'm lifting out of myself and approaching something that feels like clarity, catharsis. I fall asleep while contemplating the glow-in-the-dark constellations that dot her ceiling. Surprisingly tender for a hardhead.

*

In the morning, I walk on a cloud all the way home. Everything is glowing, reflecting off the slickness of recent rainfall. The usually dingy sidewalks have found a new freshness.

And then a pang of guilt about Chekhov gets to me. I stop by his favorite place and grab some baloney and kibble I can't afford, the organic kind that he likes. Sometimes, he'll eat so much of it that I have to massage his belly in order to ease his digestion. Just keep a hand on him while we watch interior design shows together.

My apartment has this mustiness that overtakes it when I'm away for too long. Like old cave and old cat. It also holds a hint of the tobacco stink left over from several tenants ago. It's baked into the walls. I crack a window by the kitchen and pour myself a glass of water. When was my last one? When was the last time I was out so late? When was the last time I enjoyed myself? It's all up in the air. My internal jury's frustrated, impatient, overstimulated by cheap coffee, watching the clock and wondering when we'll break for lunch.

Nothing like staying over at someone's place when they have nothing but condiments, Lipton tea, and canned soup. It's a classic fuckboy tactic, or like what producers do to contestants on *The Bachelor*. Starve them out of good judgment.

Chekhov isn't at his usual spot by the window, but I decide to fix us our favorite: Spaghetti-Os complexified with baloney and a spoonful of mustard. Tastes like Boeuf Bourguignon if you squint your tastebuds enough. It'll pair well with the Caesar salad I brought back from the conference. A bit wilted, but we'll survive. Plus, I have one of those comically giant cookies.

I absentmindedly go to fill up Chekhov's water, and notice that it splashes and overflows. I drop the container in the sink. I check the bathroom. I check under my bed. I check behind my curtain. I check behind my boxes, the couch, the fridge. No sight of him anywhere. While mentally retracing my steps from the previous day, the plausibility of it all, the "of course" factor, all of it hits me like the hangover that settles in with the morning shadows, so sudden and deep that I cancel all of my appointments and gigs and slump around the apartment and nibble on a leftover giant cookie I find in my pocket for the rest of the day, when I realize that I am no longer a person who goes home to their best friend.

I don't even mention it, when I get back to my routine of gigs, as if nothing happened. But it's when I come home that I know and sometimes repeat to myself that this feline-shaped space all around me, in the groove of my futon, underfoot in the kitchen, and that spot on my bed where my feet rest at night, not cold, but at just the right temperature, are proof that I worry about Chekhov terribly. Until then, I crack the windows open at night.

Ekphrasis II: Ouroboros

In which Tamika laments the cisheteropatriarchy

MOTHER GODDESS. forgive me for i have sinned. in her hubris, in her pursuit of human fulfillment, a bitch scorned the erotic and resorted to fallible human ego. let me speak lust's simple language and hear her limpid message: that all who purport to drink of her blessings let go of reaching, of striving, or anticipating the sacred moment when the drops trickle to your tongue. i see now, all too clearly, that a bitch hath complicated joy, looked her in the mouth with an expression of human doubt.

one thinks it takes a certain type of temperament to get intercepted at night. no, it does not. this shit is a dialectic. an atmosphere. one minute you're hanging on to a circle, you think you find yourself at the centre of it, a young pachyderm at the interior of a herd. you take yourself for a protected element, reveling in your safety, stretching out comfortably, gamboling and exposing your soft lower belly until the older stodgy elements come in and take what they see. they take the brilliance, snatch from the creativity, the intuition, the exuberance and drain it with impunity as averted eyes and hushed voices consent to your demise.

offering to the circle, a chink in the chain that was built as it was through other offerings like you, blessings like your tender gaze, you pour her a mug of water when she gets tipsy and laughs at your lisp and goofy ways. you know that she wonders if you, like she, has lain in this musty bed in the apartment with the high ceilings and the dilapidated ceiling fan that looks like it's about to fall and the mildew spots on the ceiling.

mother goddess. i beseech your forgiveness and redemption. may i find repose deep within your chthonic folds. may the cleansing waters wash over me and renew my beating red heart.

HIPCAR

In which Frantz asserts that the girl was the crazy one

HONESTY. Impact. Productivity. Courage. Accountability. Respect.

Those are the core values at Defence Construction Incorporated.

At least, that's what the website says. Never noticed it before the interview, which I killed. Got a call back, and it looks like a sure thing, but it's always good to read the particulars and fine print. Even if it's bullshit, you gotta look for anything on paper you can point to and say, "don't get it twisted" when shit goes down. Better not get mixed up in any predicaments. Man, fuck a job. But this one would just be temporary.

Hella paperwork. Good thing I have nothing to do this week except fill out the online form. Refresh. Fill it out, and then again when the internet connection times out. I knew I shouldn't have watched that last video. Sucking my cell data dry, but then again, not that many folks dial me up, except when it's the critical matter of a delivery. Otherwise,

I've got no family members, no connections for kilometres. And these suburban bumpkins don't even bother with hello. Just squint and stare you down while you walk past, like they're trying to calculate your existence.

Form turns up red. Name at birth. Gender. Two options. So they wanna know what genitalia you're born with. Form fucking timed out again. Now they wanna confirm that you're not a robot. Click through the motorcycles. Through the stop signs. The crosswalks. Hell, if I was a robot, I would be doing anything *but* applying for security clearance.

At least I can do this virtually. Last time I did this kind of thing was at the mill, and they made me come in physically. Felt so archaic. Long line at the front office. Bunch of lunkheads staring you up and down, sussing you out. Comparing themselves to each other. Stained grey hoodies everywhere. Big trucks. They think that's what being a man's all about. Try doing three surgeries in a row.

I look like Prince in my photo ID. Took a year and seven months to get a name change. My shit is solid but the guy at the counter took my driver's license, looked back at it twice, cross-checked it again with my form. Called a colleague over who looked at it and kept looking back at me, checked it again like he was fucking MacGyver.

Sure, DCI is reprehensible. But I can't let haters dictate my choices. And what about my mortgage payments? And imagine all the land one could buy. So much land. One could get a plot and start a hobby farm. Something nice you can throw some capital at. Landscape the crap out of it. Get off the grid. Build a solid shack. Grow shrubbery. A couple of friendly trees. Hide some nice stuff behind them. Leave space for a shed, maybe a greenhouse. Kick off a hydroponic operation. Pass it down to your kids.

I'm not there yet, but it's close. For now, I've been working a small patch. Seeing what I can do with the space. Condo association was all for it. Saves us on the reserve fund for me to landscape the front of the building. No issue digging it up. Grabbed some sand soil at a construction site. It's gritty but versatile. Added some manure to enrich it. It'll do the job.

I can't not blast my tunes while working. Some of the people who walk past frown at me, like they're offended, but whatever. I get this weird feeling when I'm digging, that if I sit too still and too quietly in a field, in a garden, any green space, that the worms, the beatles, and all the bugs will follow me. I'm talking about personal invasion here. As much as I respect those creatures, I get the vibe that they don't differentiate humans from a fallen tree, a stump, or a hole. Given the chance, those shits will burrow inside you like in *Alien vs. Predator*. But let's be real. Demodex mites living inside and on us. Each of us is a walking colony. You're basically as infested as a ripe corpse, but on a different scale. So you better believe I'm all about maintaining that careful balance while digging through my planters in my socks and sandals. Fuck all of them critters that try to creep up on me.

There's no fucking way I'd let that go down. Might as well lie down and die. I won't give those grubby parasites that satisfaction. That's called being done to, not doing. Plus, I'm committed to this dugout. A little plot of soil in between the parking lot and the garage. Condo manager's a dick, but at least he had the sense to leave that there. A slice of fantasy. I'll see what I can do. For now, it looks like nothing. Crappy little planter. But I'll make it work. See, I'm not the type of guy who backs down from a challenge. I come at everything with my one hundred and ten percent.

I wish these planters were farther back on the property. They're too close to the sidewalk and I'm all exposed to whoever walks by. There goes the lady from 7B, shuffling across the parking lot, struggling with her groceries. I make like I'm about to go help her, but she eyes me down like I'm plotting her assassination in plain daylight. She'd probably call security on me if I didn't make it clear that I, too, was an owner. Can't stand her type, with her see-through leggings and ugly white kids. I just turn my back to her and go on working, instead of offering to get the door. Let her help herself.

Goddam, it's hot. I'm getting overheated. I've got the most glorious mane that starts from my treasure trail right down to the goods. I like to keep it long and shaggy. Provides more depth and perspective on my junk. Nothing but a little trim every now and then. I buzzed it all off once, but it drained all my power right at the source. I felt like Samson waking up to Delilah's deception, naked and impotent until it grew back. I won't go near there with clippers anymore.

What is it about the whine of a lawn mower that makes a hot day feel even hotter? It's always some asshole who's obsessed with lawn upkeep. For what it's worth, the shaggy front yard in front of our building has a kind of swagger to it. Crumbling brick walls, stained metal fixtures, and bubblegum-stained concrete. But the overgrown weeds out front are a low-key oasis of lushness. They absorb the hard sounds of the highway, the constant clapping noises on the hardtop, just sort of muffle everything and make you feel like you're in the middle of a meadow rather than buttfuck nowhere in an industrial wasteland.

Those weeds are entire ecological communities. Miniature green cities, if you will. That's what they are. Stare long enough and you can make out the creepy crawlers that climb up stalks, from the swarm below, probably just trying to get away from the fuckery to feel the freshness of the wind. Check out the cicadas, how they're just trying to catch a vibe under the sun before it's time to crawl back down to their homes in the ground.

It's fun to look at from a distance, of course. I've got a clear view from my car, practically my second home. It heats up real nice in there, like a greenhouse. I've started growing a few lucky seeds in the cupholders. They do pretty well in the morning sun, if I leave an open container of water for moisture. Might transfer them to the condo when it gets cooler.

They're getting tall, man. Three months ago, a buddy came back from down south. Brought me back a dozen seeds. Told me there was no way to tell which of them were male or female. I told him to miss me with that bullshit. Says you can't tell which of them would grow flowers or not. I asked him how he's gonna stick that gender binary mess on something as sacred as bud. Says that's how they make the distinction between indicas and sativas, that it's a crapshoot between male and female. I told him to get fucked, but still took the seeds.

They're coming in long and strong. It's a delicate operation but I think that by the time I harvest and package them, they'll tide me over while I wait for the security clearance to go through. That way, there'll be enough to put away some pocket money and save up for a down payment on something nice and set up me and my girl out here. It's just a matter of time.

But as I said, it's delicate. Working with people is the worst. It's hell, counting on others, whether it's on the streets or in an office. Man, I can't stand the thought of chaining myself to that many people, just to get a thing done. Anytime someone makes a sudden move at the front, you get yanked into an ordeal you never predicted.

Does it get lonely, working solo? Yes. But I can't go back to teamwork. I can't go back to the days of waiting to get a call from so and so, asking me, hey, can you move this by such and such time, hey, can you spot me, or man, can you be here, or dude, can you do that. That's why I choose to focus on the production ends of the supply chain.

I guess there's plenty to keep me busy while I wait to hear back about my clearance. It'll distract me from the bureaucracy. As it is, they're crawling up and down my personal history, demanding that I spell out my government name, every damn syllable in block letters, overturning my personal history, calling people who know me, left and right, people I listed even though I don't fuck with them anymore.

*

Not gonna lie. Gardening is a time suck. Good thing there's no rush-hour traffic at this time, going to pick up Phyllie. It's smooth like the edge of a knife all the way to her favourite art supply store. This is how to live it up, driving down the highway, playing your favourite tracks on repeat, ravaging your speakers, rupturing your eardrum with that sweet bass, windows rolled all the way up. Cause damn, it stinks here, like a rat died inside my air conditioning vent.

I only roll the window down a bit when I take the exit to Cipher, and the foulest stench comes rushing in. Classic. Can't believe I used to live out here. The people are trash. The bud is trash. The food is trash. People out here wasting their hard-earned cash on plastic groceries. What the hell they put in that shit? Last time I bought a cucumber, big as a dildo, didn't have an ounce of flavour. Might as well get a Fisher-Price tea set, wash it down with an imaginary drink.

Forget that life, man. All of them, living like grass under concrete. It programs you a certain kind of way, existing on top of one another. It's so cramped that everybody's under pressure, clawing at invisible psychic needs. See that dude with the horned-rimmed glasses across the street? Seems like a well-adjusted person who's just waiting for the bus, but he's probably scanning the area to check who he can scam. Think beyond the quick grift. He's probably looking to infiltrate someone's life, probably some nice solitary lady, and then go on to cost her the best years of her life, materially or psychologically dumping on her, just because he can, until she finally realizes it and moves on. And the worst part is that he may not even know it himself. You can't trust anybody here. Not even yourself.

It's all good, as long as you lay low, mind your business. Back in the day, I used to run around, chasing girls, left and right. All under the stern gaze of well-meaning aunties. Wasn't all bad. Had a decent-sized freelance business, and a trusty stable of clients. Still, there was a time when I used to run with the wrong crowd. Trying to make a difference. Nearly fucked myself over trying to save this place. Turns out you gotta put on your own hazmat suit before trying to wrestle unwilling subjects into coveralls and safety goggles. Else you end up dead or worse.

Riddle me this: In what world would someone who's been biking since he was still suckling his mother's teat just lose his balance at the top of a cliff? Ain't no way. Sure, I mean Doudou was woke enough to select which one he wanted milk out of, bit of a late bloomer in that regard, but taught himself how to ride a two-wheeler. Not a training wheel in sight. Look ma, no hands type shit. You mean to tell me that guy just slipped and fell like the Life Alert lady? Yes, he was a little wack sometimes, a bit on the ultraist end of Kemetic Philosophy, but ain't no way.

Not to get overly conspiratorial, but there's an obvious connection between his probable assassination and the heat we were putting on the whole construction project. A whole barnyard of complicit entities. Those DCI bitches. The fat cats from the New Stockholm Development Board. The media vultures. The frigging pigs. The sheeple of Cipher who blindly believe their bullshit.

Including my own kin. I'm a self-made guy. To hell with blood family. What's biological, anyway? You can cut up a plant, graft the cutting to another plant, end up with a whole new type of greenery. Who makes the rules, exactly? My definition of family is that they're not family if they don't see you for who you are. Mine can't even look me in the eyes when I'm around. Can't stand that fake shit.

Paid parking everywhere, but you can get a free spot if you roll up to a church parking lot. Hardly anybody there, especially on weekdays. When it's locked, it just takes some jiggling of the chain off the latch, and you're good to go. No security guards. No video surveillance. Just a free place to recline and hotbox your car while waiting on your girl.

Man, it's getting late. What's she doing? Probably shoplifted too many items to carry. But I can't stay mad when I see her.

Especially not when she's wearing that off-the-shoulder top and jeans that broadcast her fat ass. She smells good too. Fills the whole car with her exquisite aroma. Like french fries and jasmine and freesia. Just like the way she tastes. Rich and flowery.

Never met anyone like that. A real one. Talented as fuck. Could make it big as an artist if she wanted. Speaks her mind. Laughs even louder. Tatted right down to her shins. That ass belongs in a museum. Nah, scratch that, she is a whole damn museum. Would be an absolute honour to get my name or face in there, even if it was just a little smudge on her foot. That way she'd never forget me. Would be a memento of me every time she paints her toenails.

Upon entering the car, Phyllie reaches inside her bra and dumps a bunch of odds and ends in the backseat. Beads and shit. Then she complains that she's hungry, so we grab an armful of guavas from Montego's on the way out. Right away, she rips into one, and goes off on a rant about ancient seed-propagating birds in Central America, vows to make me a smoothie, nectar dripping down her chin. Humming and purring like a snow leopard. I would follow her into the widest ocean, the deepest cave. Could watch her eat all day long. It would take just that one fat-cat union job to bring my plans to fruition, to spend the rest of our days roasting things for her from our garden. Nothing complicated. Zucchini. Cherry tomatoes. Potatoes. I'd take my time with them. Just a brushing of salt, pepper, and good oil.

*

I can't even lie, the burbs are usually dry as hell, but that night, Phyllie brews us a shroom tea and we go for a walkabout, and it feels like a dream. Feels like we're underwater explorers touring a desolate seafloor. Until we run into the most world-weary weeping willow I've ever met, just staring down at us, and tears immediately stream down my face. I swear to god, it's the reincarnation of Doudou, locs sweeping down and grazing the ground. That twisted face he makes when he's deep inside a smoke-induced rant. For a minute, I forget what I must look like and wrap my arms around his trunk in a tight hug until all of a sudden my face, torso, and arms are burning and it's all these red ants crawling over and biting me. That's just like Doudou. Bitchass.

*

The following morning, we're in the kitchen nursing a light hangover when I get the call. She's setting up the blender.

Guy on the line's breathing heavy, like he just ran to the phone.

"Yeah, sure. Mr. uh… Frantz. Well, we just got your paperwork back, and says here that you got a ding on your record."

"My record? Nah, man. I'm straight. That was a mistake. I spent a whole day in court last winter to get that expunged."

"Yeah, no, that's good, but it says here that it has something to do with unpaid school fees."

"Unpaid school fees? How is that a ding on my record?"

"Oh well, that stuff goes to the credit bureau, and if it goes unpaid, you're technically liable until you deal with it."

"Well, can you hold the offer while I deal with it then?"

"Yeah, well, no. That counts as a liability, so unfortunately, we can't offer you the position."

That's when she sets off the juicer, going to town on those guavas. Damn these open concept kitchens. Now I can only make out part of what he's saying.

"Yeah, unfortunately, *bzzzzzzzzzzzzzzzzzzzzzzzz*, so as you can understand, there's *bzzzzzzzzzzzzzzzzzzzz*, and so we encourage you to *bzzzzzzzzzzzzzzzzzzzzzz.*"

I cover my free ear with my hand and wait. The juicing stops just in time to hear him say, "we wish you all the best" in a way that means "go to hell, man."

She brings back two heaping glasses of frothy juice and hands me one.

"Your dose of vitamins for the day."

"Why's it purple? Wasn't it just guavas?"

"Just drink it."

We sit in the silence of the living room while she gulps her smoothie down, and then mine too.

My eyes are two big steaming holes in the middle of my face. I want to hide my face, just so she doesn't see me like this. A total loser with nothing to show for himself, nothing to offer, except a thin-walled condo in the middle of nowhere. What's the point of all this?

Without everything else, I'm just like those water stains on the ceiling, no different from that lizard-shaped one that wraps itself around the corner of the wall, and there I am, watching the clouds from the inside.

"Who was that?" she asks.

I shrug.

"Wow. Alright then."

I grunt.

"So what do you want to do?" she asks.

"I don't know… What do you want to do?"

"Smoke a little, drive around town, watch people."

"Ah really? Man, some of these people are ignorant as shit. But mostly, they just don't know any better."

Damn, if I so much as lift a finger or open my mouth, I know that I'm about to lose my shit. Best not try it. Just sit there and breathe hard. But then, she gets quiet anyway, like I slapped her.

She's like shadow and light, hunched in her chair. I don't know, but it's like she's a spirit. I'm aware of her consciousness. I think I can hear the thoughts in her head, the blood rushing in her veins. The liquid in her brain. How lush and full of life she is.

Sitting there at the kitchen table, I have the sudden urge to flip her upside down and hang her by her feet, so that I can dry her on my windowsill with the herbs, where it's nice and cool. Preserve her essence, man. Those flowers and herbs only get louder when they're dried to a near crisp. At that point, they'll last you a lifetime.

"Why are you looking at me like that?"

I shrug, look back at the water stains, which have somehow morphed into a crouching dragon. Something in me wants to explain, but there's a burning in my chest and fists that wants to just destroy everything.

We sit there in the silence of the living room.

"Let's go out." She stands up.

"Where?"

"Why don't you take me to the humpback whale?"

Forty-five minutes later, we're pulling up to the park, and to my surprise there's a crowd. Man, I hate crowds. It's like a mass staring contest. I keep my best don't-fuck-with-me face when I push through the mob.

The second we enter, I can tell how people perceive her vibe. For a minute, I look at her and see how they see her: eye makeup reaching her temples. Mouth agape in a permanent O-face. She exudes sex and joy. It transforms the quality of the oxygen around her. Fifteen minutes in, a white family at a picnic table nearby stares us down and then gets up and moves away.

It's nice having her next to me, even if people do that thing where they look at me, then look at her, then look back at me, like they're trying to math it out. Wackasses.

We find our habitual spot on the side of the hill overlooking the artificial pond. Fucking hell, this view. I hate to admit it, but it's kind of not half-bad here. Maybe the one exception in Cipher. Just as the sun starts to set and it gets violet, the pond reflects it back like a mirror. And then I get paranoid and start looking around for somebody to roll up on us with a bill to charge us for the experience. Seems too good to be true. Some shit is so nice it feels illegal.

To the back of me, there's the construction site that sounds like the noise inside my head. Wouldn't know what to do without it. To the front of us, there's a pair of majestic red pines. A lifetime of city living has made it emotional for me to just look at a tree. It's embarrassing. Meanwhile, the pines, they stand there, ignoring me as usual. Oldheads. For a moment, I eavesdrop on their conversation. Which is heated. Apparently, they don't care much for the new brood of chipmunks that scampers around them as much as tolerate them. I mean, yeah, they burrow underground and don't generally interfere. But still, it's kind of painful for them to watch those little fuckers slip and fall. Not the greatest climbers.

Goddam. And how inadequate am I? Probably, my ancestors knew how to sit there and befriend trees. They were probably lifelong chums. Or the truth is, they may have been apathetic and caught up in the boring grind of their routines, stressing over their next appointment, their next meal, its ingredients, how to come by them. Those imposed rituals probably regulated the pace of their lives. That shit is hereditary. But here I am, a lucky fucker with a minute to spare, moments I take for granted, as filler in my day that I probably won't remember next week.

Language is funny. So much happens beyond the tongue or squiggles they make you learn in school. Sidestepping my inhibition, I ask the pines what they would do if they had a mortgage to pay but no job. They scoff and ask me back if they look like they're in the business of knowing about jobs, and by the way, what the fuck happened to the elms that used to hang over yonder. I inform them gently that their buddies are no longer, probably to make room for the fake pond. They reply, oh snap, that pond is fake? I sit there, not knowing how to explain the concept of urban design to a couple of trees. My whole chest fills up with laughter or tears, I'm not sure which one.

And then I turn to her. She has a bit of shine on her nose, that I've seen her blot with rolling papers every now and then. The skin under her eye trembles just a bit. Babygirl is tired. I reach for her hand.

"Hey, you see those pines over there?"

But she pushes me away from her so hard that I roll over to the side. A couple people look at me, like I was trying to jump her.

"Damn, what's up, Phyllie?"

She looks mad as she says this through her teeth. Not even looking my way.

"The way your whole mood just shifted. Only an hour ago, you were throwing a quiet tantrum at me instead of engaging like a mature adult."

"What's the big deal? I was feeling some type of way, and then it passed. What more do you want from me now?"

"Oh, so I have to bear the brunt of your passing emotions, and then all of a sudden, it's okay just cause you decided it was?"

She's angry. I'm angry. And now I can't believe it, but I can hear myself arguing with her, from the point of view of a better version of me.

"But what'd I do to you?"

Then she turns to me and bites her pinky fingernail. I know what I did to her, but I can't explain it. I need her to explain it. It's not real until she says it.

"Is it my job to process everything for you? For someone who shuts down regularly, you ask for a lot. And I give a lot. But you ask for too much. And you never give back. You know what we call that bullshit? Emotional porosity. You're like a sponge. A useless human sponge."

"Aw shit, come on."

"Back the fuck off."

"Why are you being a crazy bitch?"

My face is just a blank void with sunken eyes. My sight blurs, while I can see that her gaze on me is sharp as ever, looking at me with disgust. What I must look like. Suddenly, I see myself for what I am: just an imposter, playing at being an adult, with all the influence of a lone insect. Truth is, she's too good for me.

A woman passes by with her dog that looks like it's meant to show off the size of her home. Large, that is. Another one passes with an even bigger dog. Shit, they must have a backyard.

When Phyllie demands that I take her to Tamika's, you would think the car ride back to my condo and back to Cipher would have been dignified and silent, but it's quite the opposite. She spends the whole time lashing out at me, back-to-back, naming each and every one of my faults like she was waiting to dunk on me this whole time. Funny thing: I want to dunk on us both and swerve into the opposite lane, right into the mouth of one of those eighteen-wheelers on the side, and put our whole relationship to rest for good.

After I drop her off, I ride back home in silence. Finally, when I get to the parking lot and shut off the engine, I don't know how long I spend raging in my car, but by the time I get out, I've ripped every single one of those fuckers out, male or female, by the root.

Extreme Close-Up

In which bad turns to worse for Maya

WHY DID THE CHICKEN cross the road? Hell if I know. How could anyone, let alone a flightless bird, even cross a four-lane road in the middle of rush hour? Any distracted fella stands to get clipped by all that traffic. Who would have thought to bisect a residential neighbourhood with a goddamn overpass? Cronyistic politicians and city planners, that's who. There's no winning when your city is a tourniquet designed to choke the flow of life.

What I wouldn't do for a sign of life from Chekhov. Every passing hour feels like a countdown to a death sentence. He's not built like that. To fend for himself on these streets like the pigeons that flock around the strip mall, lingering among cigarette butts and other detritus. If anything, he was conditioned to receive belly rubs and human-grade poultry pâté. I checked every alleyway, every porch underside, even sniffed around the dumpsters behind the chicken wings place—there's no telling where he might have gone.

Searching a familiar place exposes it differently. At the end of my street, there's a loose panel tethered by a rusty bolt to a steel rod. In the wind, it moves in a way that reminds me what it's like to live with a writer. Swing, grate, swing, grate.

Chekhov held me down. You would think we've been together forever, but my ex ditched him when she left town. I think I've paid more than my dues to the literary community by living with a writer—the ex, not the cat. There's nothing more infuriating than witnessing someone subsume your private life into text. After a while, I'm pretty sure I could hear every time that Tinashe was transforming a moment of our daily life into a scene.

It didn't matter if we were having our anniversary or a birthday, Tinashe would wake up in a cloud of melancholy every day, coming to me as a revenant from some troubled distant land. I'd entertained her for hours at a time, asking her what the deal was, trying to cajole her into a calmer emotional state, but there was no pacifying her insecurities. Anyway, that's a fool's errand.

Tinashe was like a wall of stone, grumbling over her eggs about some psychic drama, sighing that day-old coffee breath of hers in my face. When it wasn't that, she was static in front of the television or cutting up onions, agonizing over incomprehensible things. The vibration of words. The burden of memory. Sleazy hypotheticals. What first lent her an air of depth quickly got exhausting.

It was an atmosphere I couldn't stand in the long run. I require a minimum of life hygiene, a sense that things are moving. What do you do when your lover is stuck in another reality? She wasn't gracious about it either. Whether we were fucking or especially when we were fucking, I could see it illustrated on her face, a sublimation of the moment into a story scene.

When we lay there in silence, Chekhov would walk all over us, as if we were rolling hills that he needed to cross. Sometimes he would stop halfway and settle down for a while on someone's hip. Other times he would perform a jaunty dance on my shoulder until he got bored and went back to chasing invisible prey in the hallway.

I tethered myself to Chekhov when she left. If we hadn't broken up, I think Tinashe would have trapped us both in her pages. She was constantly weaving them around us. Her clothing was made of notebook pages. She scribbled into it every night while I pretended to sleep. There's no arguing with someone who wants to insinuate themselves into your life, but only to lay down in it, nothing more.

At a certain point, we just sort of stopped all verbal communication. Tinashe would send me her thoughts in writing, always in writing, which was fine, but you can understand that it's hard to grasp the subtlety of a handwritten, 10,000-word manuscript about whether we should open up our relationship with the word "DRAFT" earmarked right down the middle of its cover page. I could have tolerated her communication style if it weren't for the fact that the manuscript was later cut up and reorganized into a book-length experimental essay that got lukewarm reviews in local literary columns.

It's a bit maddening, all that, and I might have been able to weather it, had it not been for the invitation she sent me to participate in a talkback on opening night of the play that was based on it. This bitch was active everywhere, except in our intimate space.

The breakup process was arduous but necessary. I sat with Tinashe through the journaling sessions, the healing circles, the excruciating demonstrations at open mic nights. I swore to myself that never again would I let myself be taken into such a dynamic, especially when Chekhov looked up at me with those indifferent eyes of his, those pleading meows.

Even then, I vowed to take care of him as I would take care of myself, for better or worse, even when there was only one tuna can between us. I'm his ride or die, his one and only. It's this or nothing, really.

He's seen me at my worst. He has watched my sobbing self-portraiture sessions that, frankly, left my mental health in a worse state than when I'd started. I psychologically injured myself when I decided to strip naked in front of that mirror and subject myself to my own gaze.

If he were more chatty, I fear what he would have to say about me to the world.

*

The first time was an accident, a few stray clicks while I was moving my camera, that resulted in a few interesting shots, reflected in a bathroom mirror. I can't quite pass off the next few times as accidents. I have to own up to the fact that I chose to turn those spotlights on and angle my face that way, in just that particular state.

Chekhov took issue with it right away. Usually, he never leaves my heels, especially around feeding time, and yet he was nowhere to be seen, off cowering in a pile of dirty laundry. This is essentially my dirtiest secret, something Chekhov and I share: my inability to see or perceive myself with any insight or compassion. I go around looking at others but have an aversion to doing the same thing for myself. I'm a suicidal therapist, a starving chef.

Somewhere, I'd like to think that my own self-exploration could be a vehicle to greater insight, but how could I possibly justify that when the extent of my mind space deliberates whether to eat a plain burger or an all-dressed hot dog. No, but this is a serious inquiry. The burger produces methane, and the hot dog is a disgusting combination of animal parts, an unholy abomination. It must be all the chemicals they fed me as a child. I am intimately acquainted with Red dye no. 3 and Yellow no. 5, and goodness knows I love me some aspartame.

Anyway, those images may have been interesting. Who knows? But Chekhov knows better than anyone that it wasn't so much self-expression as unearned self-regard. It would be one thing if I were vying for accuracy or insight, but I'm clearly pursuing neither of those things. What I'm up to is more akin to self-flagellation. To see myself clearly, just as I am, is to mourn who I'm not. Why else would I have used a telephoto lens? My body, in all its gaunt mediocrity, is a reminder of all the beauty out there in the world. The beauty of which I am the antithesis.

*

I should have had my head examined when I accepted Zeynab's proposition to work together, to stay over. It has cost me so much time and energy, not to mention heartache and a mysterious rash in my junk.

This is how we would pass the time when we're together. Always, when we're in bed, we would argue about the film. What it was. What it wasn't. What was at its periphery. What was at its core. And we would disagree vehemently on every point. Granted, I'm a pain in the ass and I think Zeynab understood this about me from the first shoot. What started on that first night opened a whole process that I still don't quite understand.

The body knows. Every single time I've been at her place, I've clenched my butthole, waiting for the worst. It's not that she's ever said it outright, but I'm aware of the possibility that she thinks I need her too much. Maybe I'm just a dolt who's unknowingly killing her carefully curated vibes.

Once, I left a stain on a hand towel, which I meant to rinse, but by the time I went back to get it, she'd already switched it out. For that matter, I have no idea where she keeps the towels. They seem to come from an unlimited source that I can't pinpoint.

You would think they'd be in the hallway closet, but that's where she keeps a fantastic collection of dildos. You've never seen such an assortment of engorged wonders. I don't even bother participating in their selection. She's so intuitive that I know that my favorite ones will come up in the rotation, if I wait long enough.

When they happen, our sessions last from the early afternoon into the night, but it's a game of patience to wait for her to trot out the Prolapser, an eco-friendly brand that makes their dils from recycled winter jackets. A phoenix rising out of melted and transformed synthetic fibers.

The last time I saw her, she really gave it to me, and had me grappling with the fact that as much as I despise her creative choices, they always affect me to the core. One minute into it, and my vision was dilating and blurring all the objects in her room into a garbled mash of deep red and burned orange and glowing star stickers.

I've always done my best to be a good sub, but it turned out that whenever she would switch out dils or readjust her harness, a greediness would overtake me and I'd rush her, reaching for the lube, squeezing out a dollop on the tips of my clammy fingers, cinching the belt with my teeth, until she'd slap my head away.

But the best part is that she lets me photograph her.

*

There's nowhere to sit at her place so she would lay on the floor, and I would stand, shooting her from above. She had no issues lying prone while I snapped high angle shots that made her look lost and vulnerable. What was intriguing is that she seemed at home in this desolate state. She'd angle her face down, showcasing the scar on her forehead, daring me to pierce through her facade, and openly doubting that I'll find what I'm looking for.

But I'm not looking for anything in particular. My only role is to *be with,* and welcome whatever surfaces. For one, colours have a way of communicating. The undertones of her skin have a way of shifting spontaneously, like a lava lamp. Sometimes, she's blue, then she's green, and then purple. She's never the same person in photos, I swear she can shapeshift. Maybe she has no true essence. People may talk, but images speak in even greater detail. Whenever I doubt this, all I have to do is look at her again and go back to the images I have of her and compare the distance between them.

Chekhov would have spent the sessions perched somewhere, observing her, putting on a show that he was more finicky than he really is. I think he would have hated her. He was wary of anyone who isn't me or an extension of me. She wouldn't have pretended to like him either. Most people do the polite demonstration of deferring to a pet, taking a knee and offering a few weak pats, as a show of respect to the "owner." I couldn't call myself his owner, and I don't necessarily consult him to assess someone's vibe. I can decide for myself. Plus, he's not exactly impartial. I wouldn't be surprised if his long-term plan was to outlive me and survive by eating the flesh off my face someday. I remember the way he would try to trip me when I got out of the bathtub or when I was taking a Hot Pocket out of the microwave.

Could it be that I have spent so much time looking at her just to avoid looking at myself? I don't have to be or appear like anything while I study every aspect of her. And now she exists in my archive, however much I'm ready to move on.

She let me photograph her and never once asked me for any of the images. Not even a glimpse. I've filed her portraits away with all the others. That's where I know I will never lose anyone. Family members, past lovers, and long-lost friends will always be there for me.

*

I really thought this gig would lead to others, but it has been all hassle and little payoff, and here I am, back at square one. These student loans are getting out of hand. I can't even afford to work anymore. Not many clients out there are willing to give advances for transportation and all that. Best I can do now is cut up my family photos and collage them into tableaux that maybe have some aesthetic value. For now, they're just sentimental fragments.

This is why you don't mix business and pleasure.

Business is best mixed with pain.

It might be a miscalculation to go back to Ioannis and his multi-thousand-dollar deal with NSU to photograph all their conferences this year, but what else can I do, really? Just like that, dude pivoted from weddings and baby showers to symposia and panel discussions. It's barely been a few months, and already he waxes poetic on ideal podium shots, how to pose event attendees, and how to incorporate photo waivers in conference registration processes.

This is how I know Ioannis is in over his head: He no longer remembers how to smoke. The last time I shared one with him, he held the cigarette in his hand, believing himself to be smoking it, but looking off into the distance and letting it unravel into ash while muttering to me and himself about his schedule, the symposium he had the next day, the file transfer and editing session he had to handle that night, and by the way, could I assist him with that. He looked pathetic in his black uniform and nurse's sneakers, that were meant to make him look neutral, a part of the background, just another scruffy caterer.

I couldn't resist helping him out just one last time. After all, to help him would be to help myself. Not just because I'm scraping the bottom of the barrel when it comes to my savings and hanging on my last thread of credit, but because our destinies are linked. His failure is mine. Two working-class artisans who had the audacity to take a leap of faith and attend art school with a focus on studio photography, with no family money, not so much as a sneering, decrepit wealthy aunt to catch us if we fall. We are proof of each other's possibilities. I feel him as if he were attached to my ankle by a chafing rope. If ever he tumbled into a chasm of obscurity or insolvency, I would come after him. It would be my neck too.

So I strapped on my camera and snapped on a speedlight and went to the event, at which Zeynab happened to be presenting the film. I made my rounds, covered my ass by photographing all the VIPs. I slid into my familiar pattern and crouched and contorted myself every which way to capture the best angles. And all the while, I tried to avoid the auditorium that Zeynab occupied. She was giving a talk that loomed over me the more I ignored it. The more I banished it from my sight, the more it burned a hole in my peripheral vision. I couldn't bring myself to go there, knowing that she would be at the podium, dressed in all her impeccable taste, presenting like the intriguing figure that she is. I knew she was someone on the shot list that I should capture, not a make-or-break shot, but that her absence from my selection would be notable.

It killed the last flicker of my ego to enter that room and fold myself into the crowd. To them, I'm just a disruptive series of clicks along the edges that they notice for half a millisecond until their minds flutter back to the main occasion, the real deal on stage who makes sophisticated statements that they commit to their notebooks, on the backs of the programmes, in their memories, which they'll recall and repeat at dinner parties to make themselves seem more interesting.

I missed the screening, but watching her speak, projecting clearly with her stylishly halting voice, my heart sank at the thought of how close we had been while making her film, how much attention I'd lavished on those fine palm-shaped hands and that delicate throat that she was now touching to accentuate her point.

The sheer humiliation of taking in Zeynab in front of all of these people, when it had once been just the two of us, holed up in her studio, getting high on our own thoughts and pleasure and carbon dioxide. I guess I should have felt a pang of pride at having shared intimate time with the guest, but it was unbearable, how much of her gaze she focused outward on an invisible locus in front of her, just above the crowd's head, engaging a faceless public, how she saw right through me, even when I was kneeling in front of her, right below the stage. It was worse than being truly invisible. She knew about me, who I was. Just a speck of ether, a blur of ectoplasm, a fleck of nothingness at the corner of her eye.

By that point, my blood boiled so much that I lined up behind the mic in the aisle as soon as they opened the floor to questions from the audience. In my recollection, these were the words I intended to communicate to her:

"You! You present yourself as a truth-seeker. Or, at least, you come to us, having excavated an issue that affects us all, that takes its toll on the world. But have you turned the lens inward? For the sake of accountability, I just have this one burning question: Why is it that you can't go a day without fucking anyone? No, seriously. First, it was the editor. Then it was the sound designer. Not to mention the artists you met at that creative residency out west. I heard all about it. You could have been honing your craft nestled in a spacious cabin on the side of the mountain. Instead, you were boning your peers and wreaking havoc on the team dynamic, inflicting your charms on everybody, such that a fight broke out at a workshop under the guise of creative differences. You had them hypnotized, dickmatized, living under your thumb, and what's worse is that you don't even seem aware of your actions.

"Scratch that. Actually, the worst part was when you went after one of the producers and bedded him in such a way that your project is riddled with conflicts of interests. Or was it both of them? I heard that you also started fucking the other producer, his professional rival, for god's sake. You can't even call it youthful indiscretion at this point. Look at how you're pushing 40. And it escalated to such a point that you considered withdrawing from the project, which you would have done if you'd wanted to demonstrate remorse or good conscience or whatever. But not only did you not stop yourself, you went on to pretend that none of it happened. You're indiscriminate in your taste. At this point, it's a compulsion. It's a spiritual attack. It's self-sabotage. It's pathological even, this pattern of yours. What could you possibly get out of it?

"Why… just why? I mean, why go through all the trouble of devastating a professional network that you're constantly working to rebuild. Wouldn't it make sense to get on the apps and keep some semblance of a boundary, a veneer of professionalism that might ensure the longevity of your relationships. But no, you choose to fuck or fuck with everyone you work with, and when you don't, by some chaste refusal on their part of some incidental obstacle, like say, too little time or too little space, or a vigilant monogamous partner, or an impulse to protect your relationship with your own fabled partner whom we never hear about, who also happens to keep close tabs on the duration and frequency of your outings, even the ones that take place during the day, when your meetups are ostensibly above-board, occurring under the brilliant lights of a bustling downtown café, where patrons at neighbouring tables are eavesdropping.

"And yet, you still make it work. You manage to weasel your way into these scenarios, whether it's in the daytime when your clothing is still fresh, your makeup's on straight, and there is not a stray detail on your person. And it's all the worse in the evening, when gas has accumulated in your belly, your mouth is a little less fresh, and your junk starts to take on an umami flavour.

"Is this how you do it? Is this how you must get on with people, with life, though you've learned that it's a dangerous, that it leads to sensitivities and misgivings about you, hushed criticism, rolled eyes, burned bridges, cavities, gaping holes in the fabric of your constantly dwindling social network?

"And yet, there are the most desperate of people, me included, who have still chosen to work with you. Though others advised them against it. Though it's mutually toxic for the both of you. Though only catastrophe can come of it. Though it would be better to move on and find a directory of tepid collaborators on whom you will never make a move, not so much as direct a smile that never reaches the eyes.

"But if it's the warmth of a body and the intensity of a new connection that you crave, it seems like you won't rest until you've reached that damning proximity that tells you that your senses are functioning. That you know what that flinch indicates. What that sigh of contentment means. That ache you pursue. You want to know what another's skin feels like. You won't rest until you've stroked that skin repeatedly to devastating effect.

"Or is it that you're offering something? Everything you touch, you leave affected, like an anthropologist who, in observing a remote community, leaves an indelible mark. A wake of destruction. A set of sunglasses in the Amazonian rainforest. A surgeon who leaves a wedding band in the wound.

"And if you think this is your way of practicing a polyamorous lifestyle, I've got news for you: This is not it, in any shape or form. You can't jump into it willy-nilly, without involving the necessary trappings like, say, clear communication, transparency, or an appropriate degree of consent. You're just messy, is what.

"But perhaps I'm being ruthless here. Listen, I'm not a therapist, but this reads like something more inchoate, like a seepage of yourself, or a wounded attachment style. Impossible to discern what's behind it or reconcile it with the persona you project into the world. Cool, detached, curious. You never had any communication about it or shared any reflection with anyone about it. Have you seen a therapist? Would you be willing to develop any of the self-awareness or sensitivity or sense of accountability that comes with submitting your maladjusted self to a therapist, or would you prefer to remain as you are, dangerous, that is?

"Yes, bitch, you're dangerous. On any given day, right after fucking someone, it's like you shut down. You affect this blank stare, like you're truly emptied of any desire. It's like your job is done, and you just walk right out of their lives.

"Now, normally this would crush anyone, but you don't leave people with a sense of betrayal. Rather, you leave them with a sense of inevitability, as you would expect droplets after a rain cloud.

"Did it ever occur to you that there might be a way out of this sinkhole? Maybe you could find yourself a partner, perhaps a meek sound recordist who could support you and fade into the background of whatever room you enter. You could satisfy yourself with the steadying and healthy monotony of that relationship. Who knows? Maybe it could help you turn into the kind of artist who has a prolific body of work. But no, you're like a moth to a flame. You let the heat of your passions engulf your professional life and drive you into this peripatetic sexual activity, strewn with one-night stands, gossip, and bars you can't go to anymore. You've burned every bridge you ever crossed.

"But it's warmth you need, and you'll take that warmth with you on the road to new collaborators, ever more distant. Meanwhile, the ones you've discarded, yes, the accumulating community of those who know you, who've worked alongside you or in opposition to you, and who will always, out of spite, secretly disapprove of your work, whether it be its scope, focus, or angle. They will always be there to disparage your creations, works that you've brought to life with the same care as you would a newborn child, and wish to smother it before it takes its first breath."

I'm not sure what came out exactly, but it was a consolation to express myself, even if they grabbed the mic from me and forcibly removed me from the premises. It hadn't occurred to me before that point that I didn't know how to argue, not technically nor elegantly. Who would have thought that I didn't know how to fight verbally, that if presented with the opportunity and even the upper hand, that I would just flail and slap pitifully, all of this quite ineffectually?

It was also a consolation, when she finally looked me straight in the eye and acknowledged my presence for the first time that day, even if it was from the podium, and for a fleeting moment, even if I didn't necessarily see affection in those eyes, I didn't see surprise either. We were reunited in each other's field of view, and what I do appreciate is that this time there were other witnesses.

Tiger Balm

In which Mattie triggers a stormy weather front

THERE'S A RIPPLE of light on the ceiling, like the shadows cast on the bottom of a pool. I think it's a sign. Of what, I can't begin to wonder. Below my window, children play and cars whoosh past, the sound of which filters through the glass in a murmur reminiscent of the ocean near my childhood town. The last time I fell in and out of sleep, I was transported to the moment I lost my first tooth, the lower central incisor.

And yet every now and again, I hear the familiar sounds that situate me in this sweltering silverfish-infested high rise. The beeping of the garbage truck. The smell of the garlic sauce rising from the shawarma place next door. The neighbour who cranks the volume of his murderous shooting games.

I've never, in all of my 15 years of incremental rent increases in this Cipher Falls building, laid on my bed in my room during the day. The mauve drapes and lavender duvet cover may have been bleached by the sun, but they cast a spectral glow on the white walls, giving it the look of a littoral cave.

It is oppressively hot, as if God Himself has given up, rolled over and crushed me with the length of His body. So I lie here with such a strong metallic taste in my mouth that I have to swipe my tongue every now and then to check for blood.

My fingers and toes feel stiff, as though they are webbed together into a long useless appendage. My skin, usually cocoa-butter smooth, feels scaly, there's no softening it. The most I can do is prostrate myself to this lethargy. Submit to this moment while time tiptoes across my body.

This is the first instance ever that my rent is past due. I know that because of the landlord's pestering. Whenever he wants to communicate with me, he sends his minions: thousands of bloodsucking insects who gather in the folds of my mattress and communicate dirty news on his behalf. The last time, it was a rent increase. A two-digit percent increase despite the fact that this shit talker hadn't lifted a single finger to fix a thing in this building in a decade. Worst of all, his minions spent the rest of the week reminding me of the terrible news. I had a new patchwork of bumps as a memento.

This time around, a silverfish slipped out of the shower drain and I stomped him back down with my bare feet. Imagine that. Good thing I had a washcloth on hand to cleanse myself of the viscous abomination underfoot. While I was at it, I scraped the overgrown cuticles around my toenails. And then suddenly another one appeared, just as juicy as his predecessor, and then a third, until the bathtub was teeming with them. So naturally, I stomped and stomped until they were no longer. I haven't showered since.

What makes my landlord a *tèt zozo*? It's the way he breathes on everything, the notes he leaves in the hallway, elevator, and lobby entrance, how he insists on asserting everything as his property, even as other people are paying for it. When he smiles at me, that thin-lipped *djol santi* smile, I know that his tongue is tasting the sweat of my brow and savouring every drop.

He says the apartment he rents to me is a part of his family heritage, that he would eventually like to reclaim it, that he would compensate me fairly if I left it. I am sure that the family heritage to which he refers is degraded and barbaric, to the point of inbreeding. I've seen the way he pokes his nose and licks at its contents when he believes nobody is watching. I've overheard his rambling unintelligible monotone backwoods voice. I've heard all about how he finds pretexts to perform unauthorized apartment searches and then filches little objects of value from tenants. His family heritage is nothing but a smelly rag he waves in my direction in order to drive me out.

I don't have the strength or wherewithal to cancel my appointments. That, I know because I've heard my clients rap at the door, calling my name from the hallway. I've even heard my neighbour pause his games in the adjacent room and the muffled hallway conversation, presumptuously explaining away my absence even though I'm very much here, wasting away in this compromised state.

So far, I haven't had much follow-up from any of my clients, especially not those who live near the so-called city centre and who insinuate to me that I live too far away. They'll find someone else. At a cheaper rate, even. Nobody comes to Cipher unless it's to consume us. They bottle up a specimen and come back when they need more, having categorized and described it for their enjoyment.

*

The ripple of light on the ceiling. The last time I saw it, it flared outward and hit the gold frame of a family photo in which I look like a stranger to myself. Someone who belongs elsewhere. Somewhere.

The apartment is in dire need of a wash. Nothing less than a bucket of hot water and diluted Javex will do. I would crack a window too, if it weren't for the thick layer of smog that wraps itself around the city skyline around this time of the year. It takes about ten minutes for the dust and filthy film to coat my belongings. For one, the ficus has wilted. I'm not quite sure what else to do about it. I would fortify it with menstrual blood, but that flow dried up a while ago.

A patch of dry skin is flaking around my chest and my scalp is itchy, but I've been afraid to shower. A silverfish in the corner of the tub hasn't budged for three days and I don't have the guts to investigate if it lives.

I've invested so much energy in this apartment, all for it to crumble and entomb me. Perhaps I should face the fact that I'm on a sinking ship. It has come to my attention that I nested in a mausoleum of my own creation. This isn't what I want. If I had to choose a way to go, it wouldn't be by wasting away like this. I would rather pass in my sleep or experience sudden death.

I think of Lot's wife and that fatal gesture. How she turned around and became salt before she could register any of the trappings, the trinkets, and other baubles that might have brought her pleasure throughout her fleeting existence. What a way to go—at the prime of her life, spared from the uncertainty of the ascetic road ahead, surrounded by her children and husband at the city gate, gazing back with regret at the debauchery of her former life. I too, would have turned around and immortalized that moment.

Quite the opposite of this slow wasting away on this sinking ship of a city in a one-bedroom coffin with its south-facing windows. When they inevitably find my body in these cramped quarters, I wish for them to photograph my corpse alongside my belongings and publish the prints. It will be the finest portrait of me that will have ever circulated.

Let me be explicit: I wish to be buried with my silk bedding and Egyptian cotton bathrobe. Alongside my case of fine cognac, and the crystal tumblers with which I enjoy them. Prop me on my Nigerian birthing chair and surround me with my Kente cloth cushions and matching shaggy throw blanket and outsize sheepskin rug and Portuguese mosaic tile backsplash and Moroccan puff and the Jordanian almonds from my niece's wedding and my Haitian feray wall hanging and my collection of long burning votive candles and my record player and my soul vinyl records and my prints of The Kitchen Table series and my copy of Jamaica Kincaid's *Lucy* and *The Complete Stories* of Clarice Lispector and my vintage Cazal sunglasses and my Magic Wand vibrator.

Time and time again, I have tried to express my wishes to Eileen, but that fool will probably end up doing whatever she wants. It has always been water and oil, our friendship. Funny how some of our longest-standing relations chafe the most. If you had asked me a few days ago, I would have grasped for logic, a sense of finality. Ultimately, I am at peace.

There's no telling what day or time Eileen came to visit, when she sat on the edge of my bed, eating the same powdered donuts she'd brought me. I knew it was her by the obnoxious smacking of her lips. I fell asleep and didn't see her leave, but I knew she had been there and that I hadn't imagined her annoying visit by the layer of powdered sugar she had left on my duvet. Chups.

I want nothing but joy and peace for her, whatever that means, and may it be truly hers.

There was a time, 22 years ago, when we could share a bottle of Red Zinfandel and laugh until our throats were raw. I had never felt more at ease in New Stockholm. I'd had the sense that I could do anything or enter any restaurant or cafe as I pleased. But I suppose it wasn't a geographical shift. It was and is still a confounding place. I think it was something within us.

Eileen was different back then, with her fierce take-no-prisoners approach to life. Now it's as if a pathetic creature had slithered out of murky waters and taken upon itself to speak through my friend. She used to glow with pride and fear no man. When we would flounce down the street together, it awed me that she ignored the gazes studying her décolleté as it plunged all the way down to her upper ribs. Her mean-spirited, deep-throated laugh would send pigeons fluttering off sidewalks. That is the Eileen I will always treasure and remember.

What does it take for a grown woman to lose her skin? I want to scratch the eyes out of the man who made her. He didn't make Eileen, not the one I knew. Rather, he crafted her imposter, the one who sat at the edge of my bed talking nonsense, circling around the minutiae of the latest man she's frequenting, always ingratiating herself and running after these good for nothing parasites who prey on the nearest available vessels.

But I shouldn't blame the victim. Victims don't create themselves. They are manifested out of a slow brew of curdled sorrow turned self-pity turned self-indulgence turned evil. A cellar of iniquity full of bottled-up rage and poison that can contaminate whole lineages and gene pools. As much as I try, I can't protect Eileen from him, from anyone.

There is no controlling what happens. And I don't think she shares my interpretation. Eileen is in another storyline entirely. What's more, she's hard-headed. She doesn't often let me touch her delicate head of hair, but the last time I sat her down in front of me, there was no getting through to her scalp. Try as I might, the comb wouldn't pass. It was a futile exercise. I settled on a shallow blowout, tried to do what I could with her split ends, which I clipped and moisturised. Beyond that, I gave up. Anything else on my part would have been coercion.

In another life, I wonder if Eileen and I would have been lovers. After all, don't we share the same proclivity for beautiful objects? Back when we were closer, I would have been happy to exit this life, empty-handed with my two long arms. But of course, there are other times I'm not so cavalier. When I lay in my bed, hearing the swarm of activity above and below me. I am convinced that the curtain of smog and spit that envelops the people of Cipher Falls is just a toxic fog of excess. I think of Granmè Jean-Louis, and how she lived to be 109 years old in Jacmel, perched up in the crest of the hills of citrus groves, nestled in the crisp mountain air. You should have seen how deeply she would squat to pick up a fallen orange. She was quick witted enough to swat a young fly without breaking the flow of an anecdote. Her forehead was as smooth as the wood that composed the house.

How embarrassed she would be to see me huff and puff up these stairs. How I struggle lately to exfoliate my back. How rough the soles of my feet have become since I've not been able to reach them. If I were to take my ancestors as a reference point, is there a measurement system for how long it should take to, say, fetch bread and milk and spices for breakfast? When someone says they are going to run around the block to deliver paperwork, how many hours should that last?

*

I've finally managed a brief shower.

Afterward, I douse myself with a protective spritz of Chanel no. 5. In that liquid blessing, I could leave the house buck-naked and would still feel elegantly dressed. Eileen says I should ease up on it, that the quantities I wear are suffocating. I say let her choke on my good taste.

I must have passed out right after. When I awoke, it was from a dream that I was in a hospital bed. Someone had changed me into one of those paper-thin gowns and I couldn't tell where they had stored my silky housecoat with the flowers embroidered along the hem.

In those first moments of waking, I thought it was garbage day again, and that a week had already passed. Now as I sit in my darkened apartment, the air feels bone-chillingly damp. My stomach is empty and there is nothing to eat except the last of Eileen's powdered donuts, which have turned into something reminiscent of hard knuckles.

I turn to the stove to heat some water, and while I scan the kitchen for something to boil, a glint in the kettle startles me.

Between the sunken eyes and the deep lines etched around the mouth, my reflection recounts my pain. She beholds disappointment and whispers accusations to my face. No matter how much I command Her to hush, She hisses words that pierce me to my core, harsh words of someone who knows all too well how to scrape me from the inside out.

Worst of all, She seems gratified by the opportunity to break my bones and suck their marrow. I shake my fists to the kettle and raise my voice and hear myself screech, until my throat and lungs burn like I'm underwater. But She won't stop, so I continue screeching, and ignore the water boiling on the stove as well as the neighbour's pounding on the wall while I threaten to shatter Her into a million silent pieces. She hardly flinches. Laughs instead and dares me to do it. As if I wouldn't.

As if I wouldn't pluck those hard eyes out. As if I wouldn't scrape those frown lines deeper. And just then, it occurs to me that I could cause a scene. With just a gesture, I could go back to my room, lay down indefinitely, and create my own sense of finality. Eileen could have a field day, centering herself in the story of my demise, sporting her best hat at my burial, running her mouth about how she'd brought me pastries in my final days. Pastor Joseph could ascribe me to the theme of his next sermons, thrusting me into the hearts and minds of the community, a cautionary tale that would bring any wayward youth back on the straight and narrow path.

But it won't be so. And so, I reach for myself.

When I slip off my bonnet, pull out a matted cluster of hair, my heart aches with grief for all the lost time. But all I know is that I must keep going.

When I moisten my hair and part it in neat rows for the first time in who knows how long, my hand falters from lack of use. All I know is that I must keep going.

When my hands start to shake as I tie the first knot around a strand, I doubt my ability to grip it from the root. All I know is that I must keep going.

And while my hands continue braiding, eventually, my mouth buttresses the effort by humming the refrain that little Mahalia sang in church. And while my fingers twist and turn upon themselves, each time they grasp strand after strand after strand after strand after strand. Who knows how long I sit like this, but, gradually, before I know it, more substance slips through my fingers, starting with the stale air of my apartment, and then the walls and their smooth painted surface, then the drywall, and all its mites, silverfish, and crawlers, then the steel beams along with the insulation, then the wooden scaffolding, and even an empty den of mice burrowed deeply for years, and the layer of brick slips into my clutches while I carry on this way, knotting a rhythmical pattern of threads, until the whole building and the neighbourhood, the adjacent ones that compose New Stockholm, all its atmosphere, slip into my sway.

As far as my neighbours are concerned, I am merely the sour-faced woman who lives in apartment 302, the one who braids and knots and greases and braids. And I don't pay them any mind, I just continue my business not knowing where it leads. My hands respond to a powerful cue in the pit of my stomach, while the rest of my body facilitates this inward winding motion, reorganizing the elements around me.

That is not to say that everything I hate suddenly disappears. On the contrary, all those loathsome elements—the smog, honking horns, careening city buses, mean-spirited passers-by, and fresh dogshit on the pavement—are all very much still present, except that now they fold into my palms, emerge from my finger transformed, that is tightly bound around each other, reorganized, to my heart's content.

Looking out my window, I note that the muggy weather has evolved into wind gusts, billowing clouds, and darkened concrete. Of course, I have no plans to leave the apartment today. There's no telling how long I can or will continue my process. For now, I know that it pleases me, that there is nothing else I care to do, that I've ordained my hands to press on in this motion, but only just as long as this pattern brings me peace.

The Screening

In which Chekhov and the townsfolk regard the pain of others

An atmospheric disturbance over Cipher Falls triggers a storm system. Gusts of wind ruffle the tree branches in a borough developers have renamed after a project that concerns nobody but themselves. In the lobby of a renovated theatre in downtown New Stockholm, a cat slinks in the shadows while two latecomers plead with a box office employee in the hopes of finagling seats for a screening that was sold out only a few days after it was advertised. Welcome to the latest edition of the New Stockholm International Documentary Film Festival, nicknamed "Niss Diff" by habitués. No chance in hell they're getting in. Not at this point of the night, when the room is filling up with so many colognes and a concealed tuna sandwich that snuck in with the audience.

You've never seen someone fuss so much over the arrangement of chairs, but the production team was guided by a stage hand with some knowledge of semiotics and feng shui who spent no less than 25 minutes placing, replacing, and removing the cluster of chairs on stage, assessing the configuration they'd discussed in the production meeting, to optimize the ambience of the coming Q&A discussion. First, she set the chairs in a straight line, but when that seemed too stiff, she created a small semi-circle, which blocked the camera angle for the guest filmmaker who would be seated at the edge of the stage, and then back to the straight line formation, only to end up, at the suggestion of the sound guy, creating a slight semi-circle with the moderator's chair on the opposite side of the stage. But that created a distancing effect between moderator and panelists, whereas the original goal was to create an easy breezy atmosphere. Just as she was about to give up, she opted to place a jaunty coffee table in the gap between the chairs, a solution that gave it a convivial living room effect. A vase of hydrangeas on the table added a splash of grace.

There is infighting within the programming committee. Among the handful of gatekeepers, a faction believes that the best way to organize a festival is by forming a makeshift community, hosting it as an ephemeral living room space in which the public can gather and see itself reflected. For this, they turned to a historic venue, a 230-year old theatre in which a 19th-century politician was shot in the head while enjoying a vaudeville act.

The other faction believes that the festival space, embedded as it is within the material world, is simply a platform to display cultural products and encourage their consumption. That much is clear, given how much effort is dedicated to garnering grants and sponsorship deals. How else does one pay artists' fees? As formally opposed as these perspectives are, there was never any open disagreement between the parties. The tension simply manifests as an unsettling atmosphere.

When the panelists reach the stage, they take their assigned seats in the setup. The lighting on stage is perfect. It highlights each participant and their carefully chosen outfits. One can't help but notice that Zeynab is wearing an understated outfit, her trusty uniform, a hijab, military trench, her favorite slacks, and worn-out leather boots which strike the right note between nonchalance and can-do attitude. Her makeup highlights her dashing face. The whole getup announces: this person is tasteful yet unafraid to get tangled in the weeds of life.

The moderator arrives fashionably late, draped in silky reflective fabric like a magician-for-hire, carrying a notebook filled with notes about their latest quests and obsessions, absolutely ready to pontificate to any bystander about the energetic dimensions of filmmaking process, an extensive subject about which they're passionate. They also come with questions, longstanding questions that have plagued them about performance studies and cultural theory and another bundle of disciplines that have ensnared them into a life outside of the bounds of practicality, into a perpetual whirlpool of investigation.

By the time a northerly wind picks up enough speed to drop the temperature, the Niss Diff programme kicks off the screening with a series of punchy shorts. The first features the filmmaker eating a bowl of soup while staring meaningfully into the camera. The second short ups the ante with an intervention where a swarm of bees is unleashed on a naked man in a see-through tube. As the bees envelop his body, the man points an indifferent gaze into the distance, camera left, leaving the viewer to relate to his pain, or not. The third short is a thematic variation of the first, except that it relies on voiceover to drive a point home about the filmmaker's emotionally unavailable grandmother. To varying degrees, all the films in the series grooms the audience's receptivity to the feature film titled "Momentum: Voices from the Underground," which has been promoted far and wide in the community and much anticipated.

As the images appear on screen, so does a process of deep hypnosis—for some, including the cat, who has found a cosy hiding spot in a corner of the auditorium. One individual seated front row centre can't stand the distracting way their friend breathes too heavily and snorts-laughs at the wrong things. Some others have trouble getting hooked, are still too preoccupied with life beyond this temporarily darkened room. They sneak peeks at their phones, despite their seatmate's admonishments that you can't take them anywhere.

Hard to pinpoint what the audience perceives in tonight's screening. To some, it's just stimulation, a series of flickering frames, distressed images, grainy textures, all of which hold only as much meaning as the visions that bloom in the back of their eyelids. To the cat, it's the faint ambient chirping of birds and insects in the audio background. It's really up to each spectator's own imagination. Some of them had dreary visions, others had lofty sights, and still others were happy to take life as a binary or, at best, a gradient between primary colors.

All that can be said is that when Zeynab's film finally comes on, there is a shared feeling of dread among the expectant audience. Dread that usually comes to them when they are asked something about themselves, which is how they interpret this work. It's about them. A 90-minute interrogation that will ask them to shift their understanding of the residents of Cipher Falls.

This dread is possibly exacerbated by the low moan of the soundtrack, that sound design, somewhere between a roar and a hum, that disrupts even the most rigid of moviegoers. It could also be due to another notable aspect of the work: Zeynab's physical mediation. She's left traces of herself in the film, with every off-screen mumble, in car reflections, in the way the interviews are set up, their intimacy, the intensity and freshness of the emotions that the subjects reflect back on screen.

When at last Doudou's inanimate body appears on screen, someone lets out an involuntary shriek that pierces through the quiet. The shriek is silently understood as a legitimate critique that voices a collective visceral response in the tightly packed room. Prompted by that cry, someone in the front row tries to whisper an analysis to their seatmate but is hushed back into silence.

While the audience takes in the film, some wonder, who and where are the subjects? That's to say, the good people of Cipher Falls featured on screen, their loved ones, the community, those whose realities are being interpreted. There are exactly three people from the neighbourhood in the room.

And when the last frame darkens, the crowd lets out a breath. As the closing credits crawl down the screen, some of the more dutiful audience members squint at the production details, to orient their understanding of the film. Meanwhile, the cat has fallen asleep with a paw draped across his face. Others rush to put on their jackets and grab the overdue smoke they've been craving for the last hour and a half.

These folks will come back, ten minutes into the Q&A portion, in a gust of outside air and tobacco smoke, wondering about the change in atmosphere, until they finally get a whispered update from their movie companion while the more vigilant ones will contemplate the stage and catch on immediately to the dynamic. Scalpels have been drawn.

The evening's moderator, enticed by the film's abstruseness, can't wait to dissect it, expose its fleshy parts on stage. With a surprising aggressiveness, they spring right into the discussion.

"Why show us Doudou Laguerre's dead body? Don't you think it reifies violence?"

Everybody waits to hear Zeynab's answer, and she trails off for a moment and looks out beyond the crowd. When she answers questions publicly, she has a habit of holding silence and staring off at a point above everyone, blowing an energetic hole through the back wall with the intensity of her gaze. Every now and again, a confused audience member cranes their neck and turns around to check behind them.

"What do you mean by 'reifies violence?'"

"I mean, the violence that you deal with in your work. How do you show its impact, you know, reclaim an incident without subjecting people to its original pain?"

At that, Zeynab stops and clasps her hands together, a sort of conciliatory gesture, like she is pleading for mercy.

"Hmm... Original pain? What is the original pain? Don't we all share suffering? In a way, the suffering of the people of Cipher Falls isn't only theirs. Whether now or a century from now, it will still resonate in people's bodies. And if, by showing the violence they go through, my film makes someone uncomfortable, well, at least they're sharing the emotional impact, to a certain degree."

"But why do you have to show the moment of impact? What exactly are you trying to do with that?"

"What I'm trying to show is how something might make one feel, to develop a spectator's capacity for empathy."

"How do you know what is felt?

"Well, that is the question of having empathy, isn't it?"

"But what do you do about the violence felt by the people who mourn Doudou, and actually have to go through it with their bodies and spirits, not to mention those who may not know him but might still feel the effects of that which he was fighting, reckoning with the potential demolition of their community, not to mention those who lived on the land before. Where does that harm go?"

"Well, that's what catharsis is for. It's in the way I try to… restage events, I try to provide an opening through which people can reclaim the narrative, relive them and find an exit wound. Otherwise, you see, the violence is like an embedded bullet, ricocheting endlessly around the body's soft tissue, creating—no—compounding the damage and boring near irreparable holes inside the body."

Zeynab holds her own. There is something about the sensual nature of her metaphors and the offhanded way she deploys them that makes it hard to look away.

"And who is the body in this analogy?"

"Well, that's the people, of course. They're not so much a unified entity as my analogy suggests, but it's the people nonetheless."

"And who are you?"

"What do you mean, who am I?"

The moderator looks out into the crowd and pauses to identify the quadrant in which there was a scoff of indignation, before doubling down on their line of questioning.

"Who are you, in this analogy? The bullet? The gun?"

Zeynab lets her eyes rest on the vase of hydrangeas. Three beats pass before she makes a final statement against a slight screech of feedback from the microphone.

"I'm the exit wound."

The soft hum of the mic fills the room as the statement lands on the crowd.

Is that an accent? I can't place it. Did she pick it up elsewhere? Someone in the front row could've sworn she has never set foot south of the border. Two friends in the back row guffaw at her pronunciation of the word "wound" like "wund."

How did she mean it? Did she mean to say it that way?

And those two friends in the front row will argue for weeks about the slant of her statements, whether it encompasses her worldview or was a simple provocation. The energy and intensity of their arguments will eventually impact their trust and fragilize their burgeoning relationship.

But Zeynab does not care and, if she hadn't meditated for 20 minutes before taking her seat on stage, imagining something like a large protective flower that intercepted negative intentions, or hadn't taken the spoonful of honey to soften her speech as she had been advised by a root worker, or remembering how proud her deceased parents would be, just for the fact that their daughter was in this auditorium, physically elevated above the people, Zeynab would be, not exactly crying, but letting her brow line fall and losing control of her tightly pursed lips in a way that would reveal the anxiety she feels in that the moment, as she always feels when confronted by the public, a ravenous crowd that reminds her of a recurring dream she has in which a rabid mob hoists her over their shoulders and throws her off the edge of a cliff, a fate she secretly believes she deserves. But she braces herself.

Meanwhile, the most critical thinkers in the crowd furrow their brows and cross their hands in front of themselves, pumped up and ready to rant up a storm when they go out for drinks later.

If Zeynab is going to insinuate herself into other people's pain, she'd better come with an offering. Why is she indicating that there is a problem? And what, exactly, is she suggesting that they do about it instead? Of the supposed evil embedded in the structure of their lives, let her come out with it, let her be, at once, the jury and defendant, come out blameless, judicious, spotless, impeccable in her assessment of right and wrong, because that's a lot to claim. Enough to get people out of their houses on a cozy Sunday night.

And what gives her the right, exactly? To sniff around and scrutinize their lives and find them wanting? What's at stake for her? She'd better believe that hundreds of fingers will go flying to their browsers, googling every inch of her life, scrolling intently to find a point of blame, some basis on which to accuse her of bias or unfairness, a crooked path or peccadillo or misplaced word that will delegitimize her work and distort the symmetrical face she presents to the world tonight, those cheekbones that point as high as the sky, suggesting some sort of moral and technical superiority because of the fact that as they go about their mundane work lives, goofing off on the job, watching the clock, unaware of the evil in the world, for which they may or may not be responsible.

The tension is such that during the audience Q&A portion, the cat stirs from his sleep while some wacko in the crowd takes to the mic, loses all bearing, and launches into an unintelligible tirade, voice strangled by an intense knot of emotion that 1) appears to have nothing to do with the presentation, 2) is frankly embarrassing, so much so that the production assistant takes matters into her own hands and rallies two colleagues to usher the heckler out of the auditorium, to everyone's relief, at which point the moderator cracks a joke that gets everyone laughing and releases the collective tension that was caught in their throats, and finally everyone is reminded to breathe by necessity itself.

And in this alleviated atmosphere, Zeynab looks back at the crowd, and what she sees is ugly. And she thrives on ugly. Like a bottom feeder, she takes the waste, the dirt, the smut of their lives, metabolizes it into something beautiful, ineffable, that feeds the ecosystem, makes sense of their ways, in a way they couldn't do for themselves.

To know what your life means, whether it's paying your bills, participating in a supply chain, grasping for cash as you swim away from misery, is one thing. But what source fuels your life? The actuary in the middle front row. Sure, he goes into work, pays into charities, goes to biweekly therapy sessions, tries to undo the intergenerational pain that was transferred to him as a child, kisses his children goodnight. But does he truly understand the nature of what he does, the psychic pull that led him there? Is he aware that he comes from a long line of people who, in order to ward off the fear of death, devoted their lives to working in some distant parts of the death industry? The Masters of Social Work student in the left back row? Does she know that she's destined for a life of leveraging her average intelligence, repressed racism, and the co-dependency she mistakes as empathy to work in the non-profit system for the rest of her life after she wrestles with the vagaries of grad school?

That's just the way it goes. Tomorrow night, it will be a film about an insular community in the Andes that just happened to be going about their daily lives unaware that they would be watched with such fascination and enjoyment, just a two-month hike north from their corner of their world. They never consented to it exactly, when the filmmakers pointed a camera in their faces and let them sign a form that's been scanned and stashed in an old digital folder ever since.

Small as it is, the New Stockholm film industry is an ecosystem, an economy. And these people here have paid their $14 tickets to see the goods. The most watchful being the least implicated. Middle-class whites who spectate life for sport, a demographic for whom the festival organizers unconsciously, implicitly market their programs, near their playgrounds, their watering holes, the very same commercial quadrant of the city where they will dissect the evening's offerings, so as not to drag it back to their warm beds and chafe from the crumbs in their sheets. Here and now, they will undergo this momentary discomfort and then sleep on both ears tonight.

Every single person in the audience thinks they care about Cipher Falls, whether practically or conceptually. But Zeynab and her little film bother them. The supply of service, culture, blood, sweat, tears, mannerisms, otherness, and humanity that the rest of New Stockholm has enjoyed to some degree for several generations, the substance embedded within the material realm of the city, regimenting and regulating their relationships, right down to their daily lives, padding their homes, on the tip of their fingers, their tongues, commented on like the weather, stirred into their coffee every morning, placed at the center of their dinner tables, in the local papers, online, to be dissected, represented, reproduced in their art galleries, on building walls, and in this very room, has been flung back at them as an open-ended question today.

It's no accident that this interaction was planned and vetted by a committee of cultural organizers, artists, practitioners of the highest standard who, sensitive to the national conversation about equity, diversity and inclusion, kept themselves accountable to convoke outliers and singular voices in the field, precious gems like Zeynab, who can challenge, positively challenge, the status quo, by her very presence, her physical body–that vehicles for experiences and special knowledge, every inch of it capable of subverting the conventional discourse on the topic. Whoever thinks they care will just have to sit there and endure her velvety voice, for everybody's good.

And as the cat continues sleeping, the public exit the theatre, flinch, run and scatter to their homes to hide from the downpour of an unseasonable torrential rain.

Ekphrasis III: Momentum

In which Tamika condemns

A MIGHTY EQUINE beast arose over the people. a projection of their own conceit. demolishing everything in its path. to defeat it, a first faction tried to strike its surface, but each blow landed without impact. a second faction befriended the monster and plied it with a poisoned feast, which the beast only vomited. a third faction pivoted on itself and spied the shadow that projected the shadow. revised it with a horn and turned the specter into a jolly unicorn.

o daemonic mothers! what possesses one to possess another? if one traces his shadow, as with strokes of chalk at the scene of a crime, does the illustrator possess the resultant impression? does the coroner pluck and take home each organ? should one not walk away and let the rain wash the sin, end the pain, silence the wail of the crying mother?

when the spider spins her web in the crook of the branch. or the crane builds his nest on the marshy tundra. or the mole burrows into her sturdy hole deep within the field's slope. may each find solace in their respective garrets.

bless the pyramids, the spheres, the rectangular prisms. catchments of our own making. the shelters we build to find softness. or relief from the harshness of the elements. for containment. for liberation. fill and empty according to the needs of each. even the child who has about-faced and crept back into the womb. may our castles endure or crumble according to your divine timing and wisdom.

and may we stop feasting on the dead, dear ancestresses. why should their bodies be preserved from putrefaction and propped up to the sky? is this not a perverse spectacle dedicated to the sky gods? please, o mothers, may our loved ones rest and return to the soil, and nurture the cycle of life.

jesus christ died & came back for this pu$$y

(Eww, desperate.)

In which the erotic proves useful to Phyllida

CLUSTERS OF CLIFF swallows' nests resemble boobs, somewhat alien-like, the way they're embedded on the side of this overpass. Tamika set up a pop-up studio at the spot where the kids go to skate. Constant stream of cars and exhaust and honking when there's congestion, which is all of the time. There's no plumbing, of course, but she's got enough disinfectant to sterilize her equipment.

She's blasting an ouroboros on my shin. As the needle bites into my bone, the ratatat of wheels on concrete rises above the machine's buzzing and the swallows flutter to and fro according to a mysterious rhythm. A hypnotic one. I think birdwatching is my new thing.

Not much else to look at while lying on my side, except for a few puddles from a recent downpour. One of them offers the undulating reflection of the towering high rises behind us. It calls to mind a parallel world, down below, that I wish to visit. One where giant blurry swallows flit across the sky and buildings twerk with joy.

And then a cop car creeps by and some of the kids scatter. Tamika does her best to look legit and permit-holding. Keeps her back to them while shading the part where the mouth gobbles the tail. Bijou is the only one among us who's unbothered. I guess they're drowsy from all that milk. Almost too serene. Every now and again, Tamika has to pause and shoo birds away from their bassinet.

*

Huge mistake to swing by The Dunbar. There was a hopped-up Saturday night crowd, hissing and clamoring for more fries, more nuggets, more grease. The line wrapped itself around the front window. Other than Maria, no one I know is working, but I notice a few of the regulars. Maria looks even more wired than I remembered her.

I grab a lukewarm cheeseburger to go. There's a new girl at the counter who looks like she just woke up in hell. The appliances in the kitchen are beeping off the hook. They look understaffed and the counter girl looks so frazzled I leave a tip in the box, which might be for disaster victims, but at least it's a gesture. The whole time, I had to hold my breath to avoid gagging.

Once, I thought I spotted Ted in the metro, pushing through the turnstile just as I was exiting. Hard to tell if he smiled back at me—his face looked like a giant oatmeal cookie, features remixed and awfully textured. None of the remarks I thought I wanted to say to him came to mind. I would have called out hey, but then again, only out of habit.

That week, I had a dream in which fry orders were backed up. A mob of clients held Maria hostage and threatened to impale her with a mop if I didn't hurry up. I was sweating up a storm in front of the deep fryer, trying to catch up. Ted came up from behind and yelled in my ear. He reached into the oil and fished out his dick. It was crispy golden brown. Browned to perfection.

*

Mom asked me to bring her a combo on the way to the hospital. That's the last thing I want to do, but I oblige, knowing that at least I can swipe a little something from her medicine tray to tide me over.

I can tolerate the crowded hospital smell. It's just the infection control protocol that wears me out. My armpits are sweaty and my breath is strained by the time I reach Manman's gurney. When I offer her waist beads as a get-well-soon present, she grumbles that she isn't going to wear no fetish garments. In my heart of hearts, I know that I should leave it at that, but I press on and explain that she could always also wear it as a necklace or bracelet.

And then as soon as I try to demonstrate how it works, she flings her burger at my head.

It's a mystery where she gets the strength, but she's screaming at me, just like old times, even though she looks sleepy as hell. The nurse on duty waits politely for Manman to finish yelling before drawing the cubicle curtain.

"Keep it up and you'll pop your damn stitches," I mutter while I pack up the waist beads and the rest of my things.

On my way out, as I lean in to kiss her cheek, I notice the outline of the spot where she removed a mole the old fashioned way, with twine wrapped around it to choke off the blood supply and kill it. Ultimately, I respect Manman's self-revision, and I quite liked the way that mole provided a reference point for me to look at when I can't meet her eyes.

*

I can't get enough of this ouroboros. It's healing up well, wending its way from my shin toward my calf muscle, but very much staying the course and closing the loop. To show it off at Tamika's gathering, I wear a sheer bubble-wrap sundress, showcasing my raised and prickly leg hairs even though it's pants weather. One of the newer collective members remarks as much. Like, we get it. You don't like joy.

While members trickle in, Tamika hums a tune and puts the finishing touches on an octopus that starts at a girl's lower back and stretches across the hillock of her ass. Each tentacle wraps around her buttocks like hands clasped in prayer. The girl, she's lying on her stomach, face down, identifiable only by her bum and back. They're a marvel. They're sublime. Both the ass and the art.

The girl attached to the ass says it must be nice to live off your art. Tamika says that being an artist is a euphemism for just doing whatever the hell you want. The thing is that all I think about is beading and sex stuff. She says the latter is an art form too, except that people weirdly refuse to pay good money for it.

All the while, Bijou squirms on my lap. They are definitely getting stronger. Balancing them on my knee is no longer the dainty gesture it used to be. A backbreaking undertaking. And then I don't see it coming when they snatch the string out of my hand and all the beads spill to the floor in a clatter. I needed a break anyway.

*

Maybe out of remorse for assaulting me with a burger, Manman calls me up to apologize for all those times she whipped us when we were kids. I used to believe her when she said it hurt her just as much as it hurt us. Even if her wrists were strong and spritely. Even if she knew just how to give it that extra flick to aggravate the sting. For all her able-bodied fury, she looked exhausted from a long day of eating shit from the hands of disgruntled clientele at the New Stockholm municipal service center. I think it aggravated her to see her teen daughter chilling on the couch, eating cereal for dinner in front of the TV on her hard-earned couch. But I forgive her. I was just born in the wrong place at the wrong time.

Manman says she prays for me that I won't end up in hell. I'm not sure where she thinks she'll end up, but I wonder if we're meant to take some space from each other, now and in the afterlife.

I can't imagine losing her, but then again, we were always lost to each other, even while sharing a skin and face across time and space. What's more, I only have this hide to play with, seventeen square feet or so, no bigger than Frantz's powder room. And yet, so much work lies ahead. Guess I just have to mourn the fact that I can't join her in the kingdom of heaven, nor can she join me in hell, although my invitation still stands.

*

Frantz used to watch me paint my toenails a shade called Cranberry Passion. The trick is to keep the strokes broad and to not apply them more than twice. Once, he asked me if I was aware that I talk in my sleep. That I even make decipherable sentences. I asked him how he knew that, and he said, I don't know, I guess I'm a lighter sleeper than you. I asked him if it bothered him. He shrugged. My pinky toenail came out smudged.

I figure that if I take the 9:50 am bus, I can probably make it to his condo by lunch and we could drive back to the bay and I could let him make amends by eating me out in his car. A foolproof plan.

What's the difference between an oak tree on the side of the highway and an oak tree in the middle of a city? Does one of the two feel itself to be more essentially tree-like? Seems like I could answer a lot of things if I figured out the answer to that mystery.

On the bus, I dream that the guy seated next to me fingered me in my sleep, so I punch him in the side of the head as soon as I wake up. Just in case. There's no way to know it didn't happen.

God, the burbs are way different when you don't know anyone. Or have a car. And when you think a kind stranger is stopping to help you, it's a self-deputizing lady in business casual asking you if you're a resident of Pine Crescent. I rang his phone 12 times since I've been here but haven't seen any sign of him. I bet he's stoned out of his wits right now, gibbering to himself and his plants.

*

Tamika warned me that whenever they get together, it winds up in a brawl or group sex. Sometimes both. Even so, it takes me by surprise when, all of sudden, they're yelling and bumping into each other. It's a literal clusterfuck of arms, asses, and elbows. Someone grabs my braids and pins me against the wall. But they ask first. Consent always.

Nothing like a bed with mystery stains. I reckon it gets used every time some rookie wants to join Tamika's collective. A casting couch of sorts. It takes me approximately ten instances of attending their parties before I'm invited to join in.

I have what you call anatomical intelligence. I can locate a nipple, even through several layers of clothes. This plays out as my strength when I'm in the mix. All I have to do is shimmy my arm forward and give a solid tug.

Later in the séance, I spot Octopus-ass girl in the cuddle puddle and inch closer to her to reintroduce myself. She twists to show off the piece.

"Oh my god! How does it look?"

"Time has done it well," I nod.

We compare Ouroboroses.

*

All I remember from last night is that Tamika poured me a big glass of water and cackled at the way I pronounced the word "temperament." My head spinning as I laid in the musty spare bed and watched the squeaky ceiling fan twirl. It looked like it could come crashing down any minute.

They keep Polysporin in their disgusting bathroom cabinet. I apply a dime-sized amount on my temple where the braid is ripped out. I rifle some more through the cabinet and spot a bottle of something with a worn-out label that could be Advil. Can't be certain. I take a couple to quell the throbbing pain in my head.

If there's one thing Tamika knows how to do, it's how to make a killer breakfast from motley shoplifted goods from the farmer's market. I joke that we should wife each other up and start a commune. I think I meant it.

*

What do you call it when the group meals are so regular that everyone gets on the same digestive schedule? The bathroom line swells every day at the same hour. We've got to keep the plunger on hand.

I mean, obviously this place wasn't meant to handle big collective shits. It gets so that you have to run into the nearest café for relief.

Can't stand those bougie assholes at the café and the way they challenge whether you've earned the right to drop a loaf in their toilets unless you've bought a turmeric latte or vegan gluten-free banana bread. Tastes like spiritual death and normalized fatphobia.

I hunch into a hovering position above the toilet seat, and pee with the door wide open. There's no toilet paper, so I repurpose a business card I found in my bag. It's either that or committing to sit on my own dampness.

While washing my hands, I check myself out in the mirror. Seems I'm due for a neck piece soon.

They've decorated the walls with strings of postcards. I wonder who's been collecting them. When Tamika comes back with our drinks, I can tell that something is off. She slams down the mugs and the table shakes.

"I am beyond done with this city."

*

I can't take all this pressure in my head. But contrary to a migraine, it radiates from the outside in, rather than the other way around. The meds come in handy. I've been popping them like breath mints since last week. Nobody except Tamika could tell that there was an issue. Not that there is a problem, but she asked me not to use them when I sit for a session. "I need you sensate," she said.

I'm plenty sensate, as it is. The smell of mould is overwhelming. At times like this, I get the urge to look up another tattoo artist, someone with an actual studio. I wonder if she knows how gross this is. I wonder if she knows that this is just a squat.

And I guess I asked those questions out loud because now Tamika has a firm grip on my chin and brings her face close to me, closer than she's ever been, and I can hear the choked up tears in her throat while she whispers, "Bèbi, what do you think this is? I'm doing my best!" while Bijou wails in their bassinet.

*

I've got a track stuck in my head. It's a dub remix of "Subteranne." A bit on the nose, but listenable. First I hear it on the radio at Montego's while we shoplift sweet potato purée for Bijou, and it comes up again while we're in a taxi we know we can't afford. The driver squints back at us in the rear-view mirror, commenting on the weather, on these strange times, trying to get the lay of the land around Tamika, Bijou, and me while we hold our breath, calculating the right intersection to duck out of the car.

*

For the life of me, I can't fathom how Frantz and them managed to break into this site. The moment we reach the gate, the floodlights turn on and just like that, Tamika, Bijou, and I are spotlit in a circus act called, "Hold up, Mr. DCI Rent-a-Cop, we're just trying to burrow our way out of this neighbourhood, which coincides with your employer's construction site: How personally aggravated are you, and how much are they paying you, really?"

*

We press on until we reach not a place but a sound. It's a thumping in our ears that we follow into a trail that leads to a prickly patch of brambles. I can also hear Tamika's breathing behind me, puffing and wheezing, as we push through. As if in encouragement, branches thwack at our ankles until we hit a clearing.

*

Tamika hands me Bijou and reaches for a lighter in her pocket. She takes her sweet time sucking on her cigarette before entering. We stand there, listening to chirping birdies. I look around and whistle back at them so hard that a bit of spittle slips down the side of my chin. And then we scrape at a patch of moss covering a metal door grate, low in the rock wall. We jimmy the latch and push open the grate. I take a good long look at the clearing before following her inside.

*

A cave is a cave is a cave. There's no circumventing it. You can't say it has good bones or that the vibes feel good or bad or medium. It's just a neutral hole in the earth. And yet, I could get used to this one. There's just enough space for us to fill with our backpacks, baby bag, shoe collection, art supplies, but, most importantly, our feelings of homesickness.

*

Housekeeping is a skill you can learn, Tamika reminds me, each time she picks up after me and Bijou. Gotta admit, the place is starting to look cuter by the day. It won't be so bad once we finish sweeping out the cobwebs and bat shit, she repeats, while going at it aggressively each morning. We should throw a party, she says, as a reward.

*

Bijou's really taken to the surroundings. They like to wake up before us all and regale us, the trees, the crickets, and the chickadees with a vocal repertoire composed of "Bitch, where's my milk, pt. 2." "Requiem for a cloth diaper," and "Untitled 4." We take in their concerts with rapt attention.

*

Sometimes I feel like I exist in between the cracks of my own life. Mechanically repeating the same banal gestures for reasons beyond my control. Or is life just made up of negative space? Maybe we're just meant to lie back and go through the motions until things get good again.

*

These are the directions, more or less: Past the DCI site, you head toward the bay, climb the trail and then follow the old train tracks, until you reach a grove of big sad oak trees. Whenever I see those, I remember that I miss Frantz. His stupid melancholic face. That clueless expression he gets whenever he's thinking about something too hard, which is almost always.

*

Bijou's intuition is unparalleled. While we were foraging berries, they wiggled and pointed us to a relatively clean-looking stream, bordered with trees, including a humongous decomposing trunk. Hollowed out and gridlike on the inside, the trunk looks like an abandoned city. That or the interior of a space shuttle. Ready for takeoff.

*

My yodelling skills are improving. The acoustics in the cave are simply next level. Sometimes I listen back and it's a poetic call and response. You gotta get the timing right or else it just sounds like a crowded metro station.

*

A late-summer mosquito lands on the juiciest segment of my thigh. The last of its cohort, it buzzes defeatedly while I snatch it with one swipe. That's one less itchy thing on my body. Still, I feel a pang of compassion for how lonely it must be to outlive your community.

*

What a way to wake up. Tamika was screaming and thrashing at me. Thought it was some sort of disaster, but it was just a ginormous hissing beetle crawling on my face. I let it out through the metal grate. What's the point? It'll probably come back in the same way it came.

*

When I get too grubby, I take a sponge bath out of one of the barrels Tamika set up to collect rainwater. I think I've got a technique down. Lather, scrub, cup the water in your palms, splash, repeat. My preoccupations in life have dwindled to the following: Where is the nearest body of water? When do I get to drink/see/bathe in it?

*

I've started stretching, just to see how it feels. Squats are my favourite. Something about crouching low for an extended period of time activates a memory of being an inanimate object in another life, a toy thing that turned and twisted in other people's hands, at times, cherished and fondled, and at other points, tossed across the room when I no longer served.

*

Stick and pokes. Tamika's been experimenting with them. Ever so gently, she jabs a praying mantis into my thigh. Pretty artisanal stuff. Kind of like cutting but more fussy? Always in search of a new project, she asks if she should cover the V-shaped mark just above the knee left over by a welt that resembles a bird in flight. I say, no, go around it. It's some of Manman's best work.

*

Bijou said their first word! It was either "bloop," "boob," or "*All paradises, all utopias are designed by who is not there, by the people who are not allowed in.*" Not quite sure. But I believe it was implied in their tone.

*

What do I bead? Whatever inspires me, really. Sometimes, it's a necklace. Other times it's a keychain, a thought, a curse, or torment, like when Manman left us with Granmè, who spent the weekend ordering us to fetch the remote control, her snuff, or the belt she uses to whip us with her arthritic wrist.

*

Tamika secured my tapestry over the cave entrance. We bickered over it while wading in the pond. I maintain that the piece is not so much for flaunting as it is a functional domestic object, while she rages on about the white supremacist patriarchal schism between domestic and artistic labour. At that moment, the wind picks up and protests Tamika's words. Next thing you know, she's eating her scarf and pulling the braids out of her face.

Back at the cave, she hammers nails into the piece, as if to further secure her point.

*

I can't believe my good fortune. Not even when we're lying next to a birch tree and I'm on my back with my legs elevated on its trunk, the soles of my feet to the sun, and Tamika's scratching away at her notebook, sketching her most ambitious piece yet. Dots and lines radiating from a hypothetical nipple, like the rings of Saturn. Not even when her focus shifts as she tries to fix a lopsided point in the circle, and my focus shifts too, because there is a gravitational pull, and then so too does the birch's focus shift toward Tamika, whose back rests on my elevated thigh, quite awkwardly, really. But there we are, two babes and one birch, swaying in and out of each other's energy fields. We are one. We are three.

"I call Holy Ghost," says Tamika, slipping into my thought stream.

"I call the Son," whispers the birch.

"Fine, I'll be Daddy then." I concede.

*

If I stretch for too long, my memories flash through my tendons and joints, like lightning. It's too much at once. They threaten to cut me in half, at which point panic rushes in, as if it could save me from floating away—head and torso looking down in dismay at a disembodied waist and pair of legs, the meaty bullseye cross-section where my stomach used to rest on my lower half. But I usually catch myself in time with the help of the birch, the graceful bough it extends my way. I grab hold of it and propel myself back down to unify the pieces with a squish.

*

Birthdays are so anticlimactic. What are you even supposed to feel? I've decided to celebrate myself the only way I can. Early in the morning, I strip off my clothes and stretch out like a snake in the grass, just at the mouth of the cave. Right on cue, the sunshine comes out to greet me. She makes love to my chest, legs, and stomach. Afterwards, we just lie there together for hours. When she finally has to go, I thank her and bid her goodbye with equanimity. Then I slither back into my nest.

*

One minute I'm doing my daily stretches, and the next I sense a flutter of presence behind me. And who else but motherfucking Frantz is standing at the grate. It's awkward greeting each other through the bars, but I jiggle the latch a few times before I get it right. We just stand there looking at each other and then he whips out a plump bag of guavas and hands it to me. A peace offering.

*

Can't believe how many people showed up! Through the rain, through the mud, tracking soggy dirt clumps all over Tamika's freshly beaten floor. All with provisions, decorations, delicious supplies, and even glow sticks. Friends. Frenemies. Ex-colleagues from The Dunbar. Someone even brought a kitty. I dressed him up by lacing an elegant bow tie around his neck. Octopus-ass girl was completely drenched, but she hugged and squeezed me so hard that she lifted my feet off the ground.

*

*

Frantz and I sneak out for a smoke, which turns into a makeout session. As he pins me against a tree, he suddenly stops in his tracks and looks at me funny.

"What is it?"

"This birch is in love with you."

*

Oh snap! That's my motherfucking song. I make a beeline for the makeshift dance floor and Tamika joins me under the fairy lights. How she dances is by lifting her arms and swinging them around in a windmill pattern. She's backlit by blue and red light that merges into a purple halo. She's my angel. My beautician. My queen. Let me be her canvas forever.

*

The rain pounds a sick beat and the walls are slick with our sweat. We're dancing like we've never danced before, just a throng of writhing bodies. We're underground, baby. I bump into someone. It's Frantz. He asks me to dance. I press myself against him and sway. The kitty cat wearing a bow slinks past our ankles.

*

A trickle can turn into a flow can turn into a cascade. When the soil can't absorb the rainwater, it has to collect somewhere. If I were a tree spirit or a worm, I would know this: Not far beyond, there's the rumble of water twisting, turning, and flooding.

*

Tamika screams. Bijou wails. We all run for the grate as soon as we hear the rumbling. That double-crossing motherfucking latch. How can so many good people's fate rest in its hands?

*

There's little to hold onto, except my tapestry, which hangs over the grate. I jump for it, fearful of tearing it, but the fabric feels secure enough for me to hoist myself and reach for the upper rungs of the grate where I just might be able to manually dismantle it.

*

As the crowd behind me cheers, in the split second that I almost have it, a thought hits me—about art as the saving power—the tapestry rips and then I come tumbling back down. The beads that I've spent countless hours threading scatter and break the cloudy surface of the brackish water.

*

Who would have thought that drowning feels like the aha moment you saw coming all along, like a swirl of pre-verbal memory from when you were curled up and suspended inside a womb?

No matter. Every moment fits into an oddly-shaped scrap in the palm of my hand that I thread into a string of reminders. Later I can hold them between my thumb and index finger and roll them over, one by one, just to enjoy the sensation.

By the time our mangled bodies turn up in the muck of the city's drain pipes, all of our beauty and brilliance will emerge as sediment, embedded in every gritty corner. As I brace for the impact of the upsurge, and twirl again and again on myself, what comforts me most is how terrible and thrilling and freeing the moment feels.

The Review

In which the jig is up for Zeynab

While the storm rages, Zeynab lolls in bed. The hours bleed into each other as she lets recurring memories overtake her. The time she was caught in a lie as a teenager. A half-truth about wanting to study anthropology after high school. The way her mother had asked clarifying questions while looking at her. Deep into her eyes, as if reading her mind. How she looked away in distress. *Nothing*, was the real answer. At the time, she had wanted to die alongside her father. Cancel the whole business of living altogether.

A world away from her present appetite for life. How sensitive she's become. She remembers the slightly sulfuric smell of the water, the moisture of the air and the clarity of the sky on the last day she met Doudou in that familiar place at Cipher Falls, just at the edge of the bay. The area won't exist for long, not in its current form. It's in what the city calls a developmental phase, which is to say a destruction phase. The New Stockholm Development Board can't believe it didn't rezone and rebrand the bay earlier. *Billboard* models tout the white skin and smiling faces of the prototypical residents of the new condos they are planning on implanting.

Doudou's hands invited her to look. He twisted them around each other in a subtle rotation that mesmerized her. Some derivative of the old Christian nursery rhyme, *here is the church, here is the steeple.* While they ate together, she imagined what it would feel like for their lives to be entwined more organically. She leaned into that feeling by bearing down inside herself, as if she were giving birth, until she felt an internal resistance that read as pain but wasn't quite that. The core part of oneself that can't reshape itself to accommodate others. This is a loose place, smaller and inconsequential. She imagined what it would be for those to be the hands she sees every day. She contemplated him with affection until he finished his last bite, wondering which of his ways would become their conjoined ways, if they shared them long enough.

During her last visits, they traced the neighbourhood together. What else was there to do but follow its pathways and linings and unintentional knots of contradiction. Starting right where they were, at its periphery, they made their way in a concentric pattern toward its nucleus. This part of the city feels cruel by design, in a way that might be incomprehensible to the average person. It would take an equal level of cruelty to understand it.

They stopped at the hill in the park and admired the view. He liked this. Looking at views, taking them in, as if he was trying to decide on something about the landscape or looking out for a distant friend. She watched him watch the landscape, trying to decipher what it was he saw.

Their journeys always ended at the bay. This mouth of a bay, teeming with life in all its forms. Whatever washes up into the lapping shore is an offering. It could be dirt, garbage, a human hand, a used condom. Over time, some of it had become part of the sand, each grain a piece of something that looked like a unified whole. It was everywhere, imperceptible, embedded in the construction of the city that was tied to this body of water.

Laying side by side in the gravelly sand, she felt his energy, how heat emanated from him. He gave off an earthy scent that harmonized with the elements around them. He was nature itself.

She watched him run and flop forward into the water. He splashed around, as if searching for something precious and knew exactly where to find it. When he came up and walked over to her, dripping wet, he nudged her notebook to the edge of the blanket to take a seat.

As the sun set, she had no plan except to sit with him by the water, in the expanding shade. When the shadow overtook them, she started to feel the wind's chilly edge.

Moments with Doudou were like a plunge into cold water. She couldn't meet him and stay at arm's length and hold onto the comfort that she could remain the same or better than when she encountered him. Engaging with him untethered her from familiar realities, but to walk away from him felt worse, and so she quietly submitted herself to the shock.

He let her watch him work. She didn't so much observe him as soak up the atmosphere of his process. She leaned back on the towel and listened to the scratching of his pencil against paper, letting its cadence lull you into a state of suspension. Eyes squinting against the wind and sun, she listened to him apply himself with a sort of envy. His devotion was poetic. That it took place outdoors felt all the more consequential.

She realized that she was just like the kind of person she distrusts: those who feel like they have to go elsewhere to consume culture. Why can't she make the thing she seeks?

Doudou told her that when he wasn't busy organizing, he could spend entire afternoons like this, at the beach, studying the sand to later reproduce it. What parts of the beach was it? Just abstractions. Rocky mounds. Textures. Light and shadow. It never occurred to him to reproduce the entirety of the landscape. She assumed it was because he formed a part of the land, reproducing parts of itself.

She liked to think that she wasn't changing the process by watching him work.

It's just the way she was around others. She carries herself with a blankness that people mistake for mysteriousness or interest. At any given point, she has nothing to say, nothing to add to the conversation, unless it's carefully rehearsed and performed. Mostly, she just sits there and mirrors the qualities that other people see in themselves, which creates a sort of mirage that suits most people, unless it unnerves them. In her dealings, she's learned that the less people want to see themselves reflected, the more they scorn her. She overcomes that dynamic by crouching deeper within herself until there is little left, minimal interference to drag down the interaction.

Playfully, she ripped a piece of paper out of her notebook and sketched a picture of him sketching. The tools were all wrong. The paper was too thin, the ink too runny. He glanced at it silently and neither complimented nor criticized it. He just accepted the fact of her creativity. She hadn't asked for feedback explicitly or even led with an introduction about what he would be seeing, just sort of turned the image to him and observed his response.

It seemed safe enough to show him her interpretation of him in this medium. On the other hand, she was much more circumspect when revealing other parts of what she considered her real work in the audio-visual realm. Once, she'd shown him a sample, and watched him watch it. Without a sense of exactly how she wanted him to receive it, she intuited his reaction.

She didn't so much represent life as circle around it, creating suggestions through fragments. In watching the piece, he felt that he was looking into an opaque reflective surface, noticing a vague reflection of reality, like the inside of a dirty spoon.

Whenever he rested his gaze on her notebook, she pulled it closer to her. She guarded it closely, and filled it with snippets of their every interaction, especially the silent ones. But she would never let him access the paragraphs she'd written about his life.

Scriptwriting. A valid exercise. Mapping out scenes. Amplifying a sound or gesture, giving it momentum and direction. Anticipating the narrative arc. The writing process doesn't end on paper. It persists with every action, trailing sentence, and continues in the editing room, as the images unfold on screen, developing connections between each other.

It's also a formality. A bureaucratic exercise regulated by deadlines and timelines meant to ensure that a project is in good standing. Sure, she files the paperwork on time but remains open to surprises, immersing herself in the moment, receptive to small gifts that wash up her way.

She didn't know why she was with him here yet again. At a time when her life should be facing outward, toward the rest of New Stockholm and its institutions, she hadn't counted on seeing him again in this space, off the beaten path. Doudou seemed equal parts amused and confused by her interest in him. As if he didn't quite understand what stake she had in his life. But occasionally, he asked about the film. And whenever he did, she would evade him with a look of understanding and deference. The trust she'd built with him was a wall of polished stone.

He took her through his favorite detour. It was a trail that sliced through prickly shrubs, vacant lots, and railroad tracks. Trash strewn everywhere. Remnants of parties littered these abandoned spaces.

The soil on the path had a quality that produced crumbly stone, which turned into gravelly sand in places. It crunched underfoot as she counted her footsteps during the long bouts of silence between them.

Later, she missed the night bus that would have ended their time together. In missing this bus, she imagined herself to be making a grand gesture toward disavowing the life that awaited her outside of this city. Suspended in this fog of free time, she dismissed the idea of taking a taxi, and walked back toward his place, pretending to herself that she was needed there. Clouds covered the sky, lending a chill to the air, although she was sweating under the layers of her trench coat.

At his suggestion, she waited for him at The Dunbar, after she told him she was still in town.

He showed up, this time with a friend, a distracted and reserved-looking guy who didn't introduce himself but nodded at her as if he was already briefed on who she was. The guy ate his meal and carried on a conversation as if he and Doudou were alone.

For a moment, she tried to engage the friend, asking him about his relationship to Doudou, but he deflected her gaze, making it clear that he didn't wish to be perceived. So, she retreated and just listened to their exchange.

There was a time when she wouldn't dare interfere in other people's lives. She had always walked upright in public places and stared straight ahead of her, avoiding eye contact, hoping to drift unnoticed in the background, no different than a ball of tumbleweed. There was something inside her that was unattainable, so much so that she couldn't reach it herself, and then she gradually let that thing inside her do the talking until it shone out and guided her. She redirected that energy outward until she was just thinking and listening publicly.

As in the case of her previous work, when she would visit the unsaleable edge of the neighbourhood she grew up in, Old Cipher Falls, the part that wasn't yet a dog park. Untouched swathes of the surface area the city insisted on refashioning. She'd encountered a house that was destined for demolition, and eventually started going down to the basement, and sitting there for lengths of time, for what reason she had no idea except that it was a house that had something different about it. It was on a morning walk that she felt compelled to first enter it, and soon she was spending more and more time there, just listening, and she also happened to have a recorder on hand, not for any specific reason. The recorder was just there as one would have their keys or lip balm or a tissue, another tool one uses to manage various experiences of the day, and eventually she pointed it at the house and kept doing that until the emptiness she felt inside fluttered, and she was satisfied. She then listened back to those sounds and released them publicly, giving it the mysterious and intriguing title "Subterrane," which meant that subsequently, people started listening to it and commenting on it, and folding and mixing it into narratives, whether musical or discursive until these house sounds started to take on a meaning they hadn't before then. She had simply been a conduit.

And if it had happened that someone else had bottled up that noise, perhaps in a more interesting way, she often wondered if they would have gotten the same traction or done the same work.

This question, whenever it crossed her mind, often haunted her, but she left it alone, and settled it by downplaying the impact of the recordings whenever they came up.

She and Doudou and his friend moved on to a nearby place where he ordered drinks to the table. She drank because there was little else she could think of doing with them. Because it's what they would have done anyway. She grabbed her glass and served herself to the brim, pretended that it would be her first and last, knowing that she would keep sipping, refilling her cup again and again as long as she was offered more. There was nothing else for her to do at that moment, little else that the present company was asking her to receive. So she kept drinking to the point that it blurred her edges and loosened her up until she felt bound to them in an improbable way, as if this is what she got up to every Saturday night, right there in this part of Cipher Falls, surrounded by the cliffs, low-lit enough to ward off patrolling cars.

For a moment, she forgot that she was there for a purpose. Otherwise, when cheap alcohol wasn't coursing through her veins, her head was usually swarming with the concerns of a host of individuals and institutions. From her producers' doubts that the story she proposed contained enough dramatic tension to sustain a narrative and budget, to the granting institution's demand that she justify the tax dollars they'd poured into her project, to scholars' beady attention to the nuance of her theoretical framework, to activists' obsession with the social and political repercussions of her framing, whichever side of it they fell on, to the policymakers' solicitation that there be enough legitimacy in her claims, to her director of photography's fussing about whether her vision contained enough aesthetic value, to her editor's worry about whether there was enough balance and variety in the visual material, to other filmmakers' watchfulness over how her experimentation with form might influence the medium, to her audience's hunger to be edified and entertained, and beyond all of these voices, the most nagging and damning fear that hangs on her neck like a noose and threatens to drag her underwater, the way Doudou might look back at her when he understood how she saw his life.

Seated in their company, drinking, and catching on just enough to their mood and references to laugh in sync with them, her heart sank with the knowledge that she was eulogizing them in real time. With each gesture of familiarity, she tightened her hold, what felt like possession, of them in an exquisite corpse portraiture session over which they had no control except for maybe a thread of influence that they exerted through personal affinity and charisma that you could intercept across class, race, and shared humanity.

Most of all, he knew how to translate himself to her, as opposed to some of the others—like this friend, for instance, who seemed frozen in time, repeating himself in a self-soothing traumatized posture that could pass for bravado. Doudou, on the other hand, modulated his speech, used self-conscious language, and expressed emotions that seemed to come less from within than from a constructed self that conveyed what anyone might have felt going through what he did, lucid and resonant, able to be seen and understood by spectators.

No matter how much she tried to coax him out of this defensive mode, he kept at it, as one grips the edges of a ladder before dropping into a body of water. But he seemed to have no intention to swim. She understood that and allowed it and felt grateful for his reticence and sermonizing and his generous lovemaking and the access to his intimate circle of friends, whom he held close to him as much as he did his own hands.

Early on, she had wondered whether, after the film's release, Doudou would allow her back into his orbit to witness him and his loved ones or if he would automatically distance himself in the same way that, truth be told, she might not pursue him as insistently and call him and think of him and depend on him, and check for his messages first thing in the morning, holding her breath for a response to her texts and emails regarding whether he can make the next shoot, and curse him in the deepest parts of herself for needing him so much in this way.

Until then, she savoured this ephemeral intimacy as they huddled together in their booth and watched his friend finally loosen up, ridiculing himself lightly to everybody's delight, as the buzz of the beer amplified their laughter.

Later, when the friend went home, she followed Doudou down their usual path, all the way to the harbour. They walked up the side of the hill. They took a shortcut that led to a hidden lookout. Careful, he said, as he clambered up a steep stretch of hill, off the beaten path, still pushing his bike. The trick is to calculate your way up before climbing past a cluster of brambles that hang off the elevated terrain that shows off the cityscape at dusk, and the layer of pollution that gives it a purple-yellow hue that bounces off shimmering waters that reflect the halogen light of the port. She could imagine how, to confront the distance below, a descending cyclist might contemplate their route. Stop. Look out. Start again, embrace the downslope.

By the time they reached the peak, she was panting from the effort. Every few minutes, a crow cawed in sharp intervals of two, like a call-to-arms about an oncoming predator.

Zeynab stood a few steps away from Doudou. Silhouetted by the setting sun at the cliff's edge, he puffed out his chest and let out a deep breath. How beautiful he was. How positively statuesque. Incongruous in this time and space like a looted artifact in a colonizer's museum. What happens to people like Doudou when they age, she wondered. His life force called for preservation.

The crow cawed again. A sound that resounded around them and called attention to the remarkable silence in this patch of woods. You almost forgot you were in the middle of a city, except that, from this vantage point, it presented itself like a postcard. Glowing dots and shimmering lines pulsating with car headlights. From this standpoint, a shiny tableau that had nothing to do with the clogged traffic, crumbling infrastructure, and frustrated lives that awaited them below.

It would take forty minutes of trudging downhill through unforgiving thicket to close the distance between them and New Stockholm's ground level. If only we could fly, she thought. Then, a moment of clarity. You can fly if you want to. All it takes is a suspension of disbelief. In art as in life. And she realized that she could give this moment meaning for the rest of her life, if she were to follow her instincts, as she usually did, with her personal and aesthetic choices, from the indifference she displayed instead of a smile, right down to the pair of worn leather boots she chose to wear that day.

So, with just a shove, Zeynab made her move. And given the element of surprise that informed the absence of resistance on Doudou's part and all the clear air that surged beneath him, what it felt like to push this man and his bike off that cliff was not far off from gearing up to move a hefty-looking box only to realize it's empty. A disappointing lack of tension. Still, she thrust him into the temporary limelight, a sort of macabre celebrity, brought on by the people in his life and hers when they learned that they could no longer perceive him in the casual way they did, knowing that there would always be a pang of guilt that their lives continued without him while he slipped into the local news cycle, shattering everyone's sense of security, affirming that they were separated by only a couple of degrees from dismal instances of violence, or accident, or the heart-sickening uncertainty of not knowing which one it was.

She didn't consider it then, that there would be months of head shaking and sighing and self-questioning before she could recede into the comfort of anonymity instead of facing the responsibility of being the person who propelled another into an irreversible fate, out of a sense of—who knows? Desperation? Ownership? Bloodlust?

But then again, she's an artist, and it figures that she would spend the rest of her life delving into the process of asking herself why she did it, and whether it was worth it.

ACKNOWLEDGEMENTS

Sometimes I wonder if a book is a baby, alien spawn, or microbial culture. While I settle the question, I want to express my sincere thanks to Esi Callender, Oli Siino, Deniz Başar, Nafleri, Naïke Ledan, Nathalie Batraville, Von & Joana Joachim, CP Simonise, Nelly Bassily, Elizabeth Mudenyo, Claire Saintesprit, Dona Nham, Leonora King, Popperino, Nadia Koukoui, the wondrous Stéphane Martelly & the powerful authors of Les Martiales, my ever astute editor Dimitri Nasrallah, the good people at Véhicule Press, each of the brilliant tattoo artists who've inked my skin–Lindsay Phylo, Tee Fergus, Oya (Jude), Sego Soleil, Katakankabin–not to mention Megan Thee Stallion, Whitney Houston, Sarah Vaughan, the Caribbean Sea, the Atlantic Ocean, the Pacific Ocean, all landbound sirens, Venus Envy, FRKY, Caravan Café, Café Velours, le Marché Jean-Brillant, the CDN Plaza, Barbancourt Rum, the wandering spiders on my ceiling, the mushroom spores that grew in the basement of Garner Crescent, as well as my sisters and my mama.

Also, a word on New Stockholm, the brainchild of Deniz Başar, collectively nurtured by a growing crew of artists and dreamers, including Fatma Onat, Ayşe Bayramoglu, and Art Babayants: Your prose, poetry, staging, and other practices have provided a way to respatialize and undermine the trappings of settler colonialism.

Thank you all for supporting me with the vibes, care, and brainspace I needed to finish this work.

A House by the Sea : A novel by Sikeena Karmali
A Short Journey by Car : Stories by Liam Durcan
Seventeen Tomatoes : Tales from Kashmir : Stories by Jaspreet Singh
Garbage Head : A novel by Christopher Willard
The Rent Collector : A novel by B. Glen Rotchin
Dead Man's Float : A novel by Nicholas Maes
Optique : Stories by Clayton Bailey
Out of Cleveland : Stories by Lolette Kuby
Pardon Our Monsters : Stories by Andrew Hood
Chef : A novel by Jaspreet Singh
Orfeo : A novel by Hans-Jürgen Greif
[Translated from the French by Fred A. Reed]
Anna's Shadow : A novel by David Manicom
Sundre : A novel by Christopher Willard
Animals : A novel by Don LePan
Writing Personals : A novel by Lolette Kuby
Niko : A novel by Dimitri Nasrallah
Stopping for Strangers : Stories by Daniel Griffin
The Love Monster : A novel by Missy Marston
A Message for the Emperor : A novel by Mark Frutkin
New Tab : A novel by Guillaume Morissette
Swing in the House : Stories by Anita Anand
Breathing Lessons : A novel by Andy Sinclair
Ex-Yu : Stories by Josip Novakovich
The Goddess of Fireflies : A novel by Geneviève Pettersen
[Translated from the French by Neil Smith]
All That Sang : A novella by Lydia Perović
Hungary-Hollywood Express : A novel by Éric Plamondon
[Translated from the French by Dimitri Nasrallah]
English is Not a Magic Language : A novel by Jacques Poulin
[Translated from the French by Sheila Fischman]

Tumbleweed : Stories by Josip Novakovich
A Three-Tiered Pastel Dream : Stories by Lesley Trites
Sun of a Distant Land : A novel by David Bouchet
[Translated from the French by Claire Holden Rothman]
The Original Face : A novel by Guillaume Morissette
The Bleeds : A novel by Dimitri Nasrallah
Nirliit : A novel by Juliana Léveillé-Trudel
[Translated from the French by Anita Anand]
The Deserters : A novel by Pamela Mulloy
Mayonnaise : A novel by Éric Plamondon
[Translated from the French by Dimitri Nasrallah]
The Teardown : A novel by David Homel
Apple S : A novel by Éric Plamondon
[Translated from the French by Dimitri Nasrallah]
Aphelia : A novel by Mikella Nicol
[Translated from the French by Lesley Trites]
Dominoes at the Crossroads : Stories by Kaie Kellough
Swallowed : A novel by Réjean Ducharme
[Translated from the French by Madeleine Stratford]
Book of Wings : A novel by Tawhida Tanya Evanson
The Geography of Pluto : A novel by Christopher DiRaddo
The Family Way : A novel by Christopher DiRaddo
Fear the Mirror : Stories by Cora Siré
Open Your Heart : A novel by Alexie Morin
[Translated from the French by Aimee Wall]
Hotline : A novel by Dimitri Nasrallah
Prophetess : A novel by Baharan Baniahmadi
A House Without Spirits : A novel by David Homel
Dandelion Daughter : A novel by Gabrielle Boulianne-Tremblay
[Translated from the French by Eli Tareq El Bechelany-Lynch]
Because : A novel by Andrew Steinmetz
Spirits in the Dark : A novel by H. Nigel Thomas
The War You Don't Hate : A novel by Blaise Ndala
[Translated from the French by Dimitri Nasrallah]
Kilworthy Tanner : A novel by Jean Marc Ah-Sen
Subterrane : A novel by Valérie Bah